Unraveled

The Tortured Soul Series

Kate Givans

Copyright 2014 by Kate Givans
ISBN: 978-0-9905199-5-9

For more information about the author, or for other titles by Kate Givans, visit http://authorkategivans.com

Dedication

This is for the fighters and survivors out there. You are not a victim to your past, but a warrior. Let this knowledge bring you peace and strength, and may the scars you carry provide you with compassion and empathy. Please remember that you can light the way and bring hope to others still fighting to escape. That you have the power to inspire others. That you have the ability to help someone find their wings, even if you're not so certain of how to fly just yet.

In loving memory of Michael Eugene Thomsen Jr.

I hope you know how much space you filled in the hearts and homes of those that loved you most. Missing you never seems to get easier, but maybe you've finally found the serenity that just didn't seem to exist in this life.
Rest in peace, baby brother.
Love you, forever and always.

Prologue

How ironic is it that adults tell children not to lie? I mean, childhood is built upon lies . . .

Santa Claus. Mad Hatters, white rabbits, and flowers that sing. Kings and queens, princes and princesses. Dragons that must be slain or live by the sea. Old ladies that live in shoes or have bare cupboards.

They call it fiction. Fairy-tales. Make-believe.

I call them lies.

Once upon a time, I believed in them. I dreamed of visiting to mystical, far-off lands, of tea time, and of painting the roses red. I was convinced magic could defy the laws of man and physics, and that wishes could come true . . . that the universe would bend to my will, if only I hoped and believed enough.

But then the veil lifted.

Magic revealed itself as nothing more than an optical illusion, a slight of the hand designed to fool the mind. Far-off lands and magical beings were only the result of someone's overactive imagination, or maybe a serious acid trip. And, no matter how much I wished to change my fate or destiny, I couldn't deny the cold, hard truth: I had only so much control over the way my life played out, and it didn't amount to much.

Everyone reaches these conclusions at some point—for most, the process is called growing up; you put away childish things and trade them for more logical, tangible things. Rarely is there a particular moment or instance in which it happens, and few can pinpoint the reason they stopped believing, wishing, and daydreaming.

But I remember everything.

I can recall the exact second fairy-tales shattered into mirror-like shards of my lost innocence. When the allure and mystery of magic died, and I felt a fool for ever believing someone could walk on water or swallow swords. When wishes—steeped in false hope and resulting only heartache and pain—turned out to be the biggest liar of them all.

It all came crashing down after months of blowing wishes on dandelions outside our home, watching and hoping as their seeds floated off into the meadow outside our home. I imagined them being carried off to some place magical—maybe heaven, even—where a wizard, or maybe even God himself, would receive them and grant my wish.

I didn't want perfect hair or perfect teeth or a perfect body.

I didn't want a pony or popularity.

I didn't care about things like that.

I just wanted my mother to live.

Surely, the wish-granter could understand that, could see just how badly I needed her. They had to know just how frightened and helpless I felt as I watched my mother's voluptuous curves wither away until she resembled a loosely-skinned skeleton. They would save me from having to hear the rattle of her last breath—breath that would no longer speak of magical lands or say goodnight. They could stop her lips—lips that used to kiss away my ouchies and kiss me goodnight and sing the most beautiful lullabies—from turning pale, cracked and blue.

Right . . . ?

Wrong.

I blamed myself at first, thinking maybe I hadn't wished hard enough. Or that maybe my wish had been selfish. I mean, shouldn't I have been more concerned for my younger siblings and how they would cope? Didn't that matter more than my own feelings, my own fears, my own pain?

Maybe that's why she died. Maybe I didn't deserve her anymore.

Or maybe whomever, or whatever, had known what I would become, knew of the awful sins I would commit, the things I would do, the people I would hurt.

Not that I'd ever wanted to do or be those awful things.

I never asked for the hand that life dealt me.

But I suppose life doesn't ask you what you can handle, so I learned how to play. I had to, really, because I quickly found myself in the middle of a game where winner takes all. A grown up-game, one that no child should ever have to play . . . yet I found a way to win.

I played my hand and never looked back.

I'd known it would come with a heavy price—a life full of secrets and lies. What I hadn't known was that the choices I'd have to make along the way would eventually turn the monster inside my head into a living, breathing force. That my refusal to feel remorse for the measures I'd taken to secure the winning hand would turn me into the devil incarnate, saved only by the sacrifices I made. And that nothing, not even my penance could save me from having to pay the price for my sins.

But I should have known.

Because the wages of sin are death.

Death of dreams.

Death of self.

Chapter One
Present Day

I shoved my foot into the floorboard of Winnie, our 1980 Winnebago. My hands, arms, and legs trembled as I fought to keep her on the road. I'm pretty sure even my brain had started seizing by the time I pulled her out onto the highway. But I didn't slow down, despite the high-revving groan coming from her engine, and I didn't look back. I just twisted my white knuckles over the steering wheel and held on for dear life.

"Did you really have to hit him *that* fucking hard?" I seethed through clenched teeth. My shoulder blades scrunched so tight, it hurt.

"Not my fault that little boyfriend of yours doesn't know when to stay down," Cole mumbled in response as he stared out the window into the black abyss. "What'd you do to the poor guy anyway?"

"I—" My mouth clamped shut; not even the jaws of life could have pried it open. I didn't have an answer to that . . . not one that made sense, anyway.

How could I have let things go so far?

How could I have been so horribly, terribly selfish?

I didn't know.

The burning ache in my chest grew and hot, angry tears ran down my cheeks, falling in thick, heavy streams that made in nearly impossible to drive. In a desperate attempt to dam up the flood, I shoved the heel of my hand into one eye, and then the other. But it wasn't working.

Cole watched me through my reflection in the passenger window, his brow scrunched in concern. Or maybe judgment. "Want me to drive?" he asked.

I shook my head in response.

I would have given anything to just crawl in the back and fall apart, but the truth was, I needed this—the road, the vibration of the wheel beneath my hands serving as a welcome distraction from the ripping sensation behind my breastbone, from the salt of my tears as they trickled down my face into the corners of my mouth and down my chin. Because I didn't have time to fall apart. I couldn't. Not now. Not ever.

Cole said nothing, gave only a quick nod in response before opening the glove box to pull out the atlas.

He knew me better than anyone. And I'm sure he knew I was pissed at him. Livid, really. But I wouldn't be for long. Couldn't be, no matter how much I wanted to. Because it's pretty much impossible to stay angry with someone you're stuck with, someone you know would have your back, even in the worst of circumstances without ever giving it a second thought. They'd do anything for you, and you'd do the same for them.

But that didn't mean I couldn't pout a while. Or that I had to talk to him.

So I didn't.

Not that I really had anything to say, anyway. This wasn't

Cole's fault. Far from it, in fact.

From the very beginning, from the moment Josh and I met, I'd known our fate, how it would all end. Not because I planned it this way, but because this was my life. The way things were. They way they'd always been. They way they'd always be. The way they had to be.

I created this life of constantly running, never being tied down to one place, never letting anyone in. That didn't mean I hadn't hoped for something better, something more, something different. I just knew that it didn't matter how far we ran or where we hid; the demon from our past would always find us, and he'd never give us the chance to build anything that even remotely resembled a "normal" life, a life full of the things that most people took for granted.

Friendships. Relationships. Safety. Stability.

A place, a physical location, to call home.

We'd done our best to work around that, tried to give ourselves and each other something worth fighting and living for by creating it within our little family; *we* became home, the three of us together. So it didn't matter where life took us, how or when or where the roads twisted and turned, or how many times we had to pick up and move. We still had each other, and that was enough.

It had to be.

Because we might not ever have anything else.

That thought frightened me and angered me, all at once. But what can you really do when every choice, every option, every opportunity has been ripped away from you? You do the only thing you can: hold onto what you have, forget about what you don't, and focus your energy on what you can control, even if that little bit of control only exists in how you react or respond to your circumstances or surroundings.

I'd been mulling that over—how little control I really had—as we pulled off the highway for gas at mile marker two-twenty-two. Well, that, and how it felt like someone had come along and filled my chest with molten lead, my eyes with sand, and my limbs with rubber; an effect of the events earlier that night, I'm sure.

"Think we should stay the night?" Cole asked, lifting up from the seat so he could dig his wallet out of his back pocket.

I closed my eyes, leaned back in the driver's seat, let my head roll back against the head rest, blew out a slow breath of air that made my lips and cheeks puff out, and tried to think logically.

I wanted to keep going.

The more distance we could put between us and Emporia, the better off we'd be. But gods only knew I wouldn't make it much further. Cole wouldn't make it very far either, not after pulling an overnight shift the night before. Add in the Midwest's penchant for closing things down overnight—everything from restaurants to gas stations—and our chances of getting stranded without a hook-up increased exponentially. That would mean no electricity and no plumbing.

Most extreme roadies would consider them novelties,

but we tried to keep things as normal as possible for Mya. That meant having nightlights, a working toilet, and heat.

Stopping really was our best option.

"Yeah, I guess we should," I said, probably looking about as tired as I sounded. "Let's fill up first, though. I'll sleep better if I know we're prepared."

If we were lucky, our demon would wait until morning, sober up a bit before hitting the road. But since weather conditions had made south our only option, and we just so happened to be on the only southbound interstate out of Kansas, he'd be close behind, heading down the exact same highway we were on, in the exact same direction. Until we found another route, another interstate, we were sitting ducks, just waiting for him to find us.

I doubted we'd have to wait long.

Judging by his silence as he exited the rig, Cole had been thinking the exact same thing. But talking about it wouldn't change a thing. It wouldn't make our situation better. It wouldn't make it any more real. And it certainly wouldn't make it any less dangerous. So, like him, I chose to move forward, refused to stay frozen in my guilt and fear and shame, and instead went to check on Mya while he filled up.

Fast asleep, legs hanging off the side of the bed, she looked as if she didn't have a care in the world, like she hadn't just been through an experience more traumatic than most adults would even dare to consider. I suppose part of it had to do with the sheer resiliency of children, but I suspected that it had more to do with the road. It lulled her to sleep every damn time, but I guess that's just how it is when you've spent most of your life pounding pavement; the sound of the tires and the swaying motion work as a soothing balm and chase away the nightmares.

Such a shame it didn't have that effect on me.

The gods knew I could go for a good night's sleep, one without nightmares, without worries of the future or visions of my past. That wouldn't ever happen, not in this lifetime. Not when the only person that had ever made me feel truly safe had been beaten and left in the dirt, thinking I didn't care, that I'd betrayed him, that I didn't want or need him.

But for as long as I had breath in my lungs, I'd make sure the road gave Cole and Mya that peace. That they never have the same nightmares I did. Never had to commit the same evils I had, and that they were never be subjected to the horrors that haunted me every moment of every day.

I just wished I could give them more.

That I could erase the bad memories and leave them with only the good. Or, at the very least, I wished I could provide them with some sort of stability—a home, a way to finally put our demon to rest. I would have done anything to give them a shot at a normal life. For Cole to have a girlfriend and a chance at college. For Mya to have sleepovers and BFFs.

But I couldn't offer those things.

What I could give were moments like this—swinging Mya's legs back up on the bed and pulling the covers up around her chin, gently pushing the strands of strawberry blonde hair out of her face, watching her sleep with a smile, knowing that, at least in this moment, we were safe. I only hoped it would be enough, that they wouldn't hate me for all they missed. That, even if the running never ended, that they'd both be okay someday. And that they'd never look back with regret. Not for themselves, and certainly not for me.

I had known my price and I would pay it again and again if she could always sleep just like this. If Cole could always be the strong, confident, protective, caring man he'd turned out to be. I couldn't have asked for anything more.

Well, I could have, but that would have just been selfish.

When the front door to the rig slammed shut, pulling me out of the swirling, depressive thoughts in my head, I jumped.

"Just me," Cole said, turning around in the driver's seat to peer at me through the cabin. He must have noticed just how wiped I felt because the corners of his eyes lifted a little with a sympathetic smile. "Go on. Lay with her for a bit. I'll find us a place for the night."

With a grateful nod, I relinquished the wheel and curled up next to Mya on the bed. Her warmth and the cherry scent of the Jolly Rancher she'd eaten earlier helped me relax a little, and within minutes, I was fast asleep, dreaming of a crooked, grimy smile, razorblade fingers, and the sick, sweet scent of whiskey.

***

Kate Givans

Head heavy and groggy with sleep, I rolled out of bed the next morning and pulled my favorite green sweater over my white cami. I made my way to the front of the rig, twisting my tangled hair into a messy bun on the top of my head as I walked. I had every intention of waking Cole up, until I caught sight of him.

He looked so damn peaceful, mouth hanging open, snoring softly, still behind the wheel with the seat reclined and his legs propped up on the dash. He had to be wiped after the endlessness of the day before.

Maybe we could afford a little bit of time to stretch our legs. Eat breakfast. Stock up on supplies for the road. Enjoy one of our few quiet moments that seemed to be so few and far between. Maybe I could even soak up a bit of sunshine and fresh air before the long day of driving ahead.

A short walk probably wouldn't hurt either.

The exercise might help to clear my head, give my brain a momentary detour from the warm brown eyes and sandy brown hair etched in my memory and along the crevices of my heart, like a brand I couldn't shake.

But when I stepped outside, I found very little in the way of walking material. "Where the fuck are we?" I asked out loud to no one but myself, turning around in a full circle to get a better look at my surroundings.

We were parked on a circular gravel path surrounded by a patch of grass with a small green building and a cattle corral on either side. A ballpark sat to the right, and there were four white buildings with boarded up windows behind me. Just past the ballpark, I could see a sidewalk with areas of concrete jutting up at odd, dangerous-looking angles.

Judging by the cars whizzing by, we were on a main road, yet there weren't any signs to indicate what road that might be. No street signs. No stoplights. No nothing, really. Just a few trees, a liquor store, a few closed down shops, and a handful of sad-looking houses.

And here I'd thought of Emporia as small.

At least they'd had sidewalks and decent scenery—tall oaks, decorated little shops downtown, beautiful brick roads . . . this place, wherever it was, reminded me of a very small Detroit, with nothing but desolation, despair, and poverty everywhere you looked.

I made my way around the gravel path, still searching for a clue as to where we were. I finally found it after passing what looked like a dried up creek—a sign listing the Blackwell Police Department as the information source for obtaining an RV hookup.

My already heavy heart sank.

We were still in the same town that we'd stopped in to gas up. That put us just a half hour south of the Kansas state line.

I couldn't fault Cole for not being able to push through, for not getting us just a little further down the road. We'd both been wiped, but still being in the same spot meant we didn't have anywhere near as much time to relax as I'd hoped. We didn't have any time, really. Not after staying the night *and* sleeping in.

And we couldn't risk another close call, not like the last one.

He'd been in the trailer, standing just feet away from me, had been close enough for me to catch a good whiff of his rancid whiskey breath. One good blow to the head and he could have knocked me out, snatched Mya, and then it would have all been over.

There would have been nothing left to fight for.

Rest wasn't an option.

We needed to get back on the road, and soon.

Chapter Two
The Past

Momma sat with me in the grass, a pile of dandelions between us. Strands of hair, made fiery by the warm sun, blew around her face in wild waves as she showed me how to link the bright yellow flowers together to create a headband.

"The trick—" she said, choosing another dandelion from the pile "—is to pull each stem through without breaking the one before it. See here?"

I bent forward, watching as she pushed the stem of the new dandelion through the slit she'd made in the one at the bottom of the chain.

"Pull here," she said, pointing to the small bit of stem poking out through the hole. "Gently."

I carefully pulled until the yellow petals of the new flower matched up with the others, just as I'd seen her do numerous times.

"You've got it," she said, her heart-shaped lips lifting at the edges in that smile that only my mother could give—one so full of pride and love, you couldn't help but feel like the most special, perfect child in the world.

These were our moments, the peaceful ones that my mother always made time for, and I loved them more than anything. But they seemed to be fewer and farther between than they used to be. I didn't understand why. I only knew it had been weeks since we'd sat together, just her and me, the sun and the wind and the dandelions.

I knew something else, too, though. That my mother hadn't seemed herself lately. The color in her cheeks had faded. The sparkle in her blue eyes didn't seem quite as bright as it used to be. And even now, behind that smile, there seemed to be a sadness that I didn't quite understand.

"Willow, what's wrong, honey?" my mother asked, setting the chain of bright yellow flowers in her lap.

"Are you sad, momma?"

Her lips pulled into a thin line, not quite a frown, but almost. "What would make you think that?"

"I hear you cry sometimes."

"Grown-ups cry sometimes, too. I cried a lot when your grandpa passed."

"I know," I said, studying my hands as I twirled one of the dandelions in the pile. "But this seems different than when you cried over Pawpaw."

With a heavy breath that lifted her shoulders, momma raised her face to the sky, to the sun. It wasn't like usual, like when we would lay in the grass and watch the clouds. But I couldn't really say how it was different.

It just was.

When she finally looked at me again, her eyebrows were pulled tightly together. "Can I tell you a secret?" she asked, her head tilted to the side.

"I thought we weren't allowed to tell secrets." It had really been more of a question than a statement.

"This is different," momma said. "I want to tell you

something important, but I need to know that you won't tell anyone, not even your brother. Promise me, Willow."

The urgency in my mother's voice frightened me, made my stomach do weird flip-flops. "I promise," I whispered, not really sure if I wanted to know anymore. But that fear started to melt away as my mother's face softened and her smile returned.

"You're going to have a new little sister or brother."

My jaw dropped.

"What do you think, honey?"

What did I think? This was the most exciting news ever!

I imagine I must have been excited when my mom announced that she'd be having Cole (if she did announce it, that is) but I couldn't remember. I'd only been three-years-old at the time. This announcement, I would remember it for the rest of my life, and I was going to be the best big sister ever. I could help with everything now—feeding, changing, putting the baby to sleep.

And I couldn't wait.

I leapt into my mother's lap and wrapped my arms around her neck. "Really?" I squealed. "You swear it?"

She nodded against my shoulder, laughing. "Yes, really."

I suddenly realized just how hard I must have been squeezing her. With an apologetic smile, I pulled back and then sat back down in the grass in front of her. But I didn't let go of her hand, her soft and perfect hand. "How much longer?" I asked, my crossed legs bouncing at the knee, a symptom of my excitement.

"Not long," she said, squeezing my hand. "Just a few more months now."

"But, doesn't your belly get bigger when you're having a baby?" I asked, looking at my mother's small stomach with confusion.

"Oh, it does. And it has, a little. It will grow a lot more in these last few months."

"Does daddy know?"

A flicker of something passed over my mother's face, but it was gone so fast, I couldn't tell what. "He doesn't," she said, shaking her head a little. "That's why I asked you to promise it would be our secret."

"You'll have to tell him, though, right?" I asked, suddenly feeling very strange about knowing something my father didn't. Why would she keep a baby a secret from him? Wouldn't he be excited to hear the news?

"Yes, I will. Soon. But for now, it's just us girls."

"But why, momma?"

The corners of my mother's eyes crinkled as she gave me another tight smile. "You know—" she took the chain of dandelions and reached up to wrap them around my head. "I think we have just enough to make a crown out of these. What do you say we finish this off and then head back home? It's nearly supper time."

Had I been younger, I might have been distracted by her avoidance. Had I been older, maybe I would have understood the reason behind it. But I was only ten, just old enough to know something wasn't right, but still somewhat oblivious to the trials and tribulations of adults.

That wouldn't last much longer.

Soon I would know more than my young, naïve, but curious self ever could have fathomed. And then I would wish I didn't, that I could go back to that place in time, rewind my life and place it on pause. But life doesn't come with a remote control. It only moves forward, and all you can do is hold on for the ride and hope for the best.

Chapter Three
Present Day

I sat at the dinette, map unfolded in front of me, sipping at my extra cream and extra sugar mug of coffee. Hot chocolate might have been my drink of choice, but days like this one required caffeine.

We had a full day of driving ahead of us, and I needed to get us off the highway we were on. But in order to do that, I needed to have at least some sort of idea as to where we were going. I hated doing that, though—planning our destination. I felt like it made us easier to track. Suspicious, I know, but I'd apparently become a little paranoid. Rightly so, considering the razorblades ripping my heart to shreds over not leaving sooner, for letting myself fall in love, and putting everything at risk.

How could I have been so stupid? So damned careless? Oh, that's right . . . Josh.

Just the thought of him triggered a pang in my chest, one so painfully raw, I was sure my heart would fall right out onto the table, leaving behind a gaping hole in my chest so deep and wide that it'd never be filled again. Not by anything or anyone. Because there wasn't a single person or thing on this earth could ever give me what he had given me, something I'd desperately needed when he'd found me on that bridge.

Hope.

As I'd stood up on that ledge that night, looking out over the water, I thought of how easy it would be to just end it all. I wouldn't do it, not as long as Mya needed me. But there'd still been this sobering realization just before he showed up . . . if I fell, there would be no one there to catch me. No one to rescue me. Only me and the sky and the ground below.

So I'd just have to learn how to fly.

Not literally, of course, but figuratively.

Josh had been the one to give me wings with his willingness to help a complete stranger, a crazy girl standing on a bridge, ready to plummet to her death—or at the very least contemplating the idea. They grew stronger as I got to know him, learned just how kind, gentle, caring, and sensitive he really was. I bloomed under his attention, his affection, his love. And for the first time in a very long time, I felt free.

He had been more than I ever could have wished for, perfect in every way.

But none of that mattered in the end—not his beautiful soul, not his deep laugh that warmed me from the inside out, not the way he loved me without question, limitations, or conditions. It couldn't, no matter how much I wanted it to. Because things with wings have to fly in order to survive.

And that's exactly what I'd done.

I only wished I hadn't left him the way I had, probably questioning everything—if I needed him and loved him, if what we had really meant anything to me at all. I'd have given anything for just another minute, to stop him before he drove away forever and tell him that it—he—meant everything, that without him, I might not have survived my stifling reality.

But if we hadn't left when we had . . .

I swallowed against the thickness in my throat, pushed back the emotion clogging up my airway as I stuffed away any and all thoughts relating to Josh.

I was only torturing myself, adding salt to my open wound.

Not that I had anyone else but myself to blame. I'd known all along that I couldn't keep him, that I would have to eventually leave my prince, my guardian angel, my knight in shining armor.

Because girls like me—the lost ones who've sold their souls to the devil—never get what they want. No, girls like me only get what we deserve . . . more heartache and pain, even when we've already had enough to last a lifetime.

***

It'd been nearly noon by the time we managed to get back on the road. Mya sat buckled into her safety belt at the dinette in the back, watching her new movie, the same one she'd watched at "Nana Jan's." Cole worked on making everyone lunch. And me? I just tried to keep my eyes and my mind focused on the road . . . but gods I hated the Midwest.

All that flat land reminded me of those old black and white cartoons, the ones where you could tell they used the same handful of frames over and over, rehashing them into a seemingly endless loop. A cow here. A corn field there. A hill every thirty minutes or so. A patch of trees or a lake about every hour.

Some folks say the Midwest has its own beauty, that there's something amazing about being able to see for miles around. Whatever. I'd take the mountains or the forests, hell, even the plateaus of the desert over this . . . this . . . emptiness. It made the minutes feel like hours and the hours feel like days.

We hadn't even made it to Oklahoma City yet—less than two hours from where we'd started—and I already wanted a nap. Not that I could take one. We needed to at least make it to Texas that day. And after that . . . I didn't know. I still hadn't decided where we'd land next.

I tried to fool myself into believing it had more to do with not wanting to make too obvious of a choice, but the ache in my chest told me differently, reminded me that my indecisiveness had everything to do with wanting to turn the rig back around and head back to Emporia.

I loved that crazy, quirky college town. I missed its brick streets and funky vintage shops and restaurants. The way the weather would turn at the drop of a hat. How no one really seemed to notice me or my eccentric style, thanks to the throngs of college students constantly coming in and out of town for classes and holidays and breaks.

Most of all, I missed Josh.

A part of me wished he could have seen the warnings for

what they really were—a way to keep that distance between us, to save him from more pain than necessary, a sacrifice of my own heart to save his. It would have made things easier on him. But he refused the see the signs, and I'd been too weak to stay away from him, too selfish to let him go when I should have. Now, all I could do was hope that I hadn't done any irreparable damage to his kind heart or beautiful soul.

Ah, who was I kidding?

I'm nobody . . . nobody special, anyway. Not someone worthy of his love and affection, and certainly not worthy of his heartache. He deserved better, that's for certain. Obvious, even. But I had underestimated just how much I needed him—the way he looked at me, the way he touched me, the way he treated me like a normal girl . . . a girl that didn't have ghosts and secrets and demons and a fucked up past.

I would have given anything to be that girl, but she didn't exist. She was nothing more than a figment of my imagination, the girl I wanted to be, one that could love without abandon, be there for him, heal his wounds and give him something worth living for, not just for a little while, but forever.

"Want me to drive?" Cole asked, startling me out of my thoughts as he climbed into the passenger seat next to me.

I swiped angrily at the hot streams rolling down my cheeks in an attempt to hide them from my overly perceptive brother . . . not that it would do me any good.

"Nah, I'm good," I said, narrowing my eyes at the road

ahead of us, fighting against the wayward tears still trying to make their way to the surface.

"You sure? Because you don't look so good."

"I said I'm fine, Cole." I shot him a sidelong glare.

"I told you not to get attached." He paused for a moment, taking a bite of the sandwich he'd been holding before continuing with a mouth full of food. "Our lifestyle permits only playthings, Willow. You know this as well as I do."

"Sorry if I don't feel like being a female version of you," I spat, the blood in my veins turned up to boiling hot without so much as a warning. "Unlike some people in this trailer, casual sex isn't on my list of priorities."

"Right, because an active sex life is so easy to maintain when I'm playing babysitter and security guard. Or have you forgotten that I don't have any more of a life than you do?"

"I never asked you to stay, Cole," I said, quieter, the fight leaving me, guilt taking its place. "You're always free to go. You know that."

We both went silent for a while, nothing but the thump of the tires on pavement playing like a soundtrack for a good five miles.

"You know I wouldn't," Cole finally said. "It's not time yet."

My throat—clogged with regret, anger, and grief—ached too much to speak, so I gave him a simple nod.

"Hey—" Cole extended his arm across the console to grip my shoulder. "A little heartbreak comes with the territory, eh? Part of being a gypsy?"

I nodded my head again, the tears seeping from the corners of my eyes blurring the road. I blinked them away, let them stream down my cheeks a bit before swiping them away with the sleeve of my sweater.

"You're tough as nails, sis. And I promise, you've got this," Cole said, giving my shoulder a little squeeze before standing and then making his way back into the trailer. Probably checking in on Mya. Or maybe just giving me space to grieve.

Either way, I was grateful. My tears wouldn't stay at bay any longer, not when I'd gone and left my heart and soul back in Kansas, and every mile I put between myself and those vital pieces of me, the bigger the gaping hole in my chest seemed to get.

Chapter Four
The Past

Something was wrong.

I could feel it in my bones. In the shivers that raked through me as my bare feet padded along the hallway's cold hardwood floors. In the way my breath hitched each time the hem of my flannel nightgown brushed against my bare calves.

Mya had been screaming more than an hour. It wasn't an ordinary scream . . . not one that I'd ever heard her make. I knew because my heart had never done that strange pitter-patter sinking thing before. And the fact that her cries had gone unattended for so long only heightened my anxiety.

Momma should have been taking care of her, holding her, feeding her, changing her diaper, singing to her . . . something. But she wasn't. No one had come to answer Mya's cries. Not while I covered my head with my pillow in an attempt to ignore the blood-curdling sound. Not when I went into the nursery to try and console her myself. And not when I finally gave up out of frustration and worry.

Something had to be wrong.

My hand shook as I reached for the door to my parent's bedroom. The doorknob felt like ice against my clammy palm. With one deep, shaky breath, I pushed the door open and poked my head in. My stomach soured when I caught sight of the empty bed, the way the covers and sheet were hanging halfway onto the floor, tangled and twisted haphazardly.

"Mom?" I whispered, more out of fear than anything.

When I noticed the light filtering from beneath the crack of the bedroom door, my heartbeat slowed a little. But only a little. There were awful, painful sounding noises coming from the other side of the door, gagging and retching so violent, I couldn't help but cringe.

"Mom, are you okay?" I asked, making my way across the room, using the light from beneath the door as my guide. When I reached it, I tapped gently on the thin, wooden door. "Mom?"

More gagging and retching.

The worry twisting my stomach into knots grew.

"Momma, please. Mya's crying. I don't know what to do."

"Just a . . .just a second."

I heard the toilet clang, as if she'd slammed the lid shut, and then the sound of water running. Finally, the door opened.

I only wished it would have made me feel better.

"I'm sorry, honey," momma said, knuckles white as she clung to the edge of the bathroom sink, sweat trickling down her freckled face. "I didn't know I'd be in here this long."

"Momma, is something wrong?" I asked, unable to keep the shakiness out of my voice. Because I already knew the answer.

"No, sweetie. I'm fine," my mother said, her colorless lips barely lifting at the edges. "Now, go on. Go back to bed. I'll take care of Mya."

I backed away, unable to look away from my mother's hunched body and bloodshot eyes. She might have said she was fine, but somehow, I knew she wasn't.

Something was very, very wrong.

Chapter Five
The Present

At a rest stop just outside of Austin, we stopped to give Mya a chance to stretch her legs. While she played out in the grass, chasing spring's first offering of butterflies, Cole and I sat at the picnic table, pouring over the map.

Well, Cole was.

I had been more focused on Mya. Her long strawberry blonde hair, trailing behind her like a cape. Her infectious laughter. The perfection of this moment, and how such a small thing could bring her so much happiness. I just hoped nothing ever took that joy away, that innocence. Because I, of all people, knew just how quickly the world could rip it away from you.

Cole rapped his hand on the wooden table between us. "Earth to Willow! You going to help me, or what?"

I closed my eyes and inhaled deeply, committing the moment to memory before turning my attention to him. "Sorry," I muttered, propping my arms on the table and then resting my chin in my hands.

"Where are we going, Willow?" he asked, the annoyance evident in his tone. "We can't keep driving around like this, with no sense of direction."

I pulled the map toward me. "I know," I said, staring at the red and blue lines, still no closer to a decision. Maybe if I stared hard and long enough, the map would simply tell me where to go.

"So . . .?"

"I don't know," I sighed, sliding the map back toward him. "You pick this time."

He didn't even glance at it. Instead, he just sat there, staring at me, waiting for me to break, to be the sister he'd always known—confident and calm, even in the worst of circumstances—for my affliction to melt away, for me to bleed out on the table in front of him . . . I'm sure any or all of the above would have sufficed.

But I didn't do any of those things. I just averted my eyes, turned my gaze back to Mya in an attempt to hide the tears burning, pooling, threatening to serve as evidence to just how okay I wasn't.

With a loud huff, Cole snatched the map off the table. "What the fuck is wrong with you?" he muttered, standing and then stomping off in Winnie's direction.

That was a good question.

I knew the answer, but he wasn't going to like it.

I didn't like it.

But then, I had done this to myself. To all of us.

Watching Mya again, I forced myself to focus on her and the reason I'd started all of this in the first place. This wasn't about me. It never had been, and it never would be. This was for her. And for Cole. We couldn't afford to waste time on my ridiculous pining, my lovesick, broken-hearted puppy dog bullshit. We had a job to do, a life to live.

And I needed to get my shit together, starting right then

and there.

"Mya! Time to go!" I called out, standing, making my way toward Winnie, to the door that Cole had slammed behind him, with a quick, confident stride.

I knew where we were headed now.

It might not have been the smartest choice, or maybe it was just another manifestation of my desperation, but it had potential. Healing potential, and not just for me, but for all of us.

"What about California?" I asked, standing on the metal retractable steps as the door I'd flung open clanged loudly against the outside of the rig.

Cole looked up from the map, silently holding my gaze as Mya skirted past me to head inside.

Terse seconds ticked by. My heart thundered away against my rib cage and my palms turned sweaty as the anxiousness coursed through me, making it feel like my head and heart might explode any second. Would he know? Would he guess? Would he shoot down my idea?

Finally, he nodded, his head bobbing back and forth, slow and easy, his lips turned down into a thoughtful frown. "Well, alright then," he said, grinning. "That's more like it."

In one deep, cleansing breath, I released all my grief and worry. Well, most of it, anyway. We had a plan, at least, and that was better than where we were just minutes before.

"Good." I stepped the rest of the way into the rig and shut the door behind me. "We'll plan the rest of our route at the next stop. Albuquerque. We've been here too long, and we need to get some miles behind us before we call it a night."

Without another word, I climbed behind the wheel, started Winnie up, and pulled through the gravel path leading back to the highway.

***

"So, California, huh?" Cole asked as I slid into the passenger seat.

He had taken over the driving so I could read Mya a story and tuck her in. We'd hit our goal of Albuquerque, but we were still going strong, had planned to try and at least make it into Arizona before we stopped for the night.

"Sounds great, right?" I asked in response, hoping I didn't sound too eager.

"Sure, sounds like a blast. The beach, chicks in bikinis . . . " He paused and slid a quick glance in my direction. "The real question is why *you're* so gung-ho about it."

My heart rate picked up a notch. "What, I can't like girls in bikinis?" I joked, internally cringing at the high-pitched sound of my own voice.

He rolled his eyes in my direction, eyebrow raised, apparently unimpressed with my sarcasm. And a little suspicious, which he had every right to be.

I hated lying to Cole, but I didn't see any good coming from telling him the truth—that I wanted to go to California because Josh had always dreamed of going. It sounded desperate and dangerous, or at least it would to my brother. To me, California gave me a piece of him, a connection.

I could spend my days roaming the streets, seeing the sights, and thinking about him, wondering how he would react to seeing the Golden Gate Bridge. What his face would look like the first time his feet touched the Pacific. Would he collect seashells? Would he throw sea stars back into the ocean? Maybe he'd build a sand castle with Mya and me . . .

Yes, California would be my sanity. My salvation. My way to keep him alive in my heart, if only for a little while.

Telling Cole any of that would only result in a change of plans. He'd stop the trailer, right there on the highway and demand I choose another location. And that'd be silly. Overreacting. Pointless, really.

Because it wasn't like Josh was *actually* going to be there.

Even if he did end up going someday, we'd probably be long gone by then. And, even if we weren't, if by some miracle we were still on the coast and he finally made the trip, we'd never see each other. California is a huge state, with lots of places to go. We could be in the same city, on the same street, and still never bump into one another. That made any concerns over my reason for wanting to go completely irrelevant.

So I lied.

"Fine," I said, shaking my head, attempting an air of annoyance. "We haven't been to the coast in ages. Not since momma was alive. And I miss it."

Cole's lips pulled into a thin line as he squinted at the road ahead, making it look as though he were trying to focus on something up ahead. But really, he was listening to me, trying to determine the validity of my statement. "That's the only reason?" he finally asked.

I was treading on dangerous ground here. Our rules—number one being brutally honest with one another—kept us safe . . . well, safer than if we completely abandoned them. Yet that was exactly what I was doing, abandoning a rule. Two, actually. Our second rule was to cut ties once we left a place and never look back.

"You're hiding something," Cole said, almost nonchalantly, as if he'd known from the very beginning that I'd been lying. .

I blew a huff of air, sending my frazzled bangs up around my head. "I'm not hiding anything," I said, swallowing against the bitter taste of the lie on my tongue. "I just want to relax for a while, take some time to breathe. What better place to do that than at the beach?"

Cole raised his eyebrows at me, but I ignored it.

"Besides," I continued. "That was a really close call—probably the closest we've ever had. We could use a place where we can get lost in the crowd, lay low without attracting attention."

"And you think Cali is the best place to do that?"

"Absolutely."

Cole's shoulders lifted and fell in a deep sigh as he nodded slowly, stiffly. "We'll need a plan before we get there," he said. "You know as well as I do, California living isn't cheap. We won't be able to survive on odd jobs and hole-in-the-wall café tips. Not out there."

"We always figure it out," I said, already hearing the waves crashing against the shore, calling my name. I couldn't have hid the smile pulling at my lips, even if I'd wanted to.

"Yeah, I suppose we do," he said, giving me a small smile back—a guarded and nervous one, but still a smile.

We were going to be okay.

I just knew it.

Even if I never saw Josh again, even if my heart never fully healed and his fingerprints forever stained my soul with their beauty, we would be okay. Because who could be sad with the sand between their toes and the sun kissing their skin?

Not me, that's for sure.

Chapter Six
The Past

"Want me to take her?" momma asked, coming up behind me and peering over my shoulder at Mya.

I shook my head and continued feeding my baby sister. "I'm getting pretty good at this."

As if she'd understood me, Mya wrapped her tiny hand around my pinky. The tiny pig-like sounds she made melted my heart and brought a small smile to my lips.

"You really are, sweetie," momma said, placing a cold, bony hand on my shoulder over the back of the rocking chair.

My feet stilled, ceasing my rocking motion as I pulled away from her touch.

"Willow?" I could hear the concern, the worry, the fear in my mother's voice.

I didn't care.

"What?" I asked, heat already building in my chest, rising up the back of my neck, heading straight for my face and ears.

Mom came around to the front of the chair, knelt down in front of me so her eyes—eyes that looked just like mine—were level with my own narrowed stare. "Are we . . . are you angry with me, honey?"

I turned my head, looked away from the deep crease in her forehead, the shimmer of tears at the corners of her eyes. She had no right, *no right,* to try and make me feel guilty for being angry with her.

She'd done this.

Forgotten about me. Cole. Mya. Slept all day instead of taking care of us. Never cooked anymore. I couldn't even remember the last time she'd read us a story, done the dishes, sat at the dinner table . . . made dandelion crowns.

This was her fault.

"Willow, honey." Momma placed her hand on my leg. It took everything I had not to jump out of the chair and put Mya in danger. "Please . . . baby, look at me."

My head rolled in her direction. I imagined it looked something like a scene out of the Exorcist . . . or at least I hoped it did. But I didn't say a word, just tried to bore holes through her head with my venomous glare.

The crease in her forehead deepened as the first tear rolled down her pale cheek. "Willow . . . I—honey—I thought I would have more time. That I could wait to tell you and your brother. Or that maybe the doctors . . . " She shook her head, as if dispelling a thought, and brought a shaky set of fingers to her mouth.

Fear replaced my anger, created a heaviness in my chest that made it impossible to breathe. I hadn't a clue where it'd come from, or why. I only knew that I wanted no part of this. I didn't want to know the words that were about to come out of her trembling lips, the thoughts swirling behind the bloodshot eyes that filled with more tears as they searched my face.

I only wanted to run, hide, pretend this moment wasn't

happening.

"Momma . . . I—"

She placed a cold hand on mine, the one that was cradling Mya's head. "Honey, it's okay. It's time for me to tell you. Past time, really. I—I should have told you sooner." She paused and swallowed so hard, I could actually see her throat moving. "Willow, honey . . . I have cancer . . . "

Momma's lips continued to move as she spoke, but nothing else quite registered in my brain. It was as though she were speaking to me underwater; her words, her tone, everything sounded so muffled. But my ears weren't the only part of my body refusing to work. My throat, it went so dry, I couldn't swallow anymore. My hands and arms and legs felt heavy, limp, useless. But they couldn't have been . . . because momma was prying Mya from my arms.

But that didn't make any sense.

I'd held my baby sister at least a million times in the past few months, months that my momma had been sick, months that she'd been fighting (and apparently losing) her battle against cancer.

"Willow!" Momma's screech burst through the water, cut right through me, shocked me back into reality. "Let go! Let go of your sister! Honey, please, give her to me. You're hurting her!"

My heart thundered so hard, I could hear whooshing in my ears as I looked down at my arms, at my mother's arms, at Mya, her little face blood red as she screamed and writhed between us.

Kate Givans

I shoved her into my momma's arms and then flew out of the rocking chair, nearly knocking both of them to the ground in the process. Something I'd never felt, never known, bubbled up my chest, into my throat, out of my mouth—a sob, so heavy, so deep, so pained, it brought me to my knees as it broke free. The green carpet, stiff and worn from age, dug into my shins and the heels of my hands as I doubled over out of fear. Fear of throwing up. Of passing out. Of losing my mother.

She was dying.

I didn't know when, and maybe I didn't fully understand what that meant just yet. Maybe, at the time, I only had the capability of realizing that she would soon be gone. Forever. And that nothing would ever bring her back. But I knew I would never forgive her for leaving us. Not when we still needed her.

When I still needed her.

Chapter Seven
Present Day

Cole released Winnie's hood and let it slam shut. "Well, we're fucked," he said, wiping his hands on a rag. "Radiator's shot. Lucky we didn't blow a fucking head gasket."

Mya tugged on the hem of my sweater. "Willow?"

"Yeah, baby?"

"It's cold inside." She rubbed her little hands up and down her arms. The pronounced pout on her lips only added to her adorable, albeit sucky, plight. "Can we turn on the heater?"

I frowned, disappointed that I couldn't do anything about the cold. Just our luck to wind up stranded in the mountains. "Sorry, sweetie," I said, running a hand through her curls. "We can't turn on the heat. Not right now."

"Is it because Winnie broke?" she asked, peering up at me with big, blue eyes.

Despite our circumstances, the side of my mouth lifted in a proud half-smile. "How'd you get so smart?" I asked, lifting her up on my hip. Lucky for me, she was still rather petite for her age. That wouldn't last much longer, though; she was starting to get heavy.

"School."

"Ah, that explains it." My grin spread at her absolute cuteness as I tapped the end of her nose with my finger before placing her back on the ground. "I'll tell you what, why don't you go inside, climb under the covers." I nodded my head in the direction of the door. "Grab the extras off the couch and I'll be in to snuggle with you in a few."

"Okay."

I watched as she went inside, intentionally stalling, refusing to acknowledge Cole just yet. Mya had this habit of picking up on and absorbing the emotions of others, like a little empath. With Cole stressed to the max, it'd only be a matter of minutes before she started panicking, too. And that was the last thing we needed, especially since I knew we'd figure it out.

We always did.

"We're not fucked," I said, finally turning to speak to Cole once Mya shut the door behind her. "We have a little saved up, and whatever we don't have, we can earn in a few days here in town."

"You're kidding, right?" Cole asked, brows tightly knit, face scrunched. "We're in Flagstaff, Willow. There isn't a damn thing around here."

"There are always odd jobs. And . . . " I turned a full circle, looking at the area around the rest stop. "There's a McDonald's. And, if all else fails, we can panhandle."

The muscles in Cole's jaw twitched as he narrowed his eyes at me. "You're out of your damn mind if you think I'm resorting to panhandling again," he seethed. "It's a fucking useless waste of time and energy. I didn't even pull half of what you did the last time, and I was out there twice as long. I got nothing but a bunch of asshats speeding by and throwing bullshit, ignorant comments at me. No. No fucking way." He threw his rag on the ground for good measure, as if I needed an even better display of just how pissed he was over being stranded with little to no money in our pockets.

"We will do what we have to do, Cole." I said, intentionally keeping my voice calm, quiet, soothing as I watched him work through the full spectrum of anger— tugging at his dark hair in the frustration stage; kicking up dirt and rocks through the pissed off stage; delivering a good swift kick to Winnie's tires, putting a dent in her fender with her fist, and then throwing an animalistic growl at the sky when he reached his complete meltdown stage.

This was my brother.

Back when we'd left home, he'd been a complete mess— acting out, raging over even the smallest things. Over the years, he'd worked hard at learning how to control it, and he could keep his cool under most circumstances. But every once in a while, when things were really stressful, he'd lose it. Then it was like watching a tornado, earthquake, and tsunami take place all at the same time.

If I tried to stop it, I would only put myself at risk. So I just stood there in silence, focusing on my breathing—in, out, in, out—as I waited for the storm to pass. Not because there weren't a million things I'd like to say swirling around in my head. And not because I was some sort of saint or Mother Theresa.

No, the only thing that kept me from speaking, from trying to do anything was that I knew Cole wouldn't ever forgive himself if I (or someone else) ever ended up hurt because of one of his rages. The guilt would eat him alive like some sick, twisted disease, like a cancer. Because, to him, he would have become his worst nightmare: our father—a man so cold, so calculating, so malicious that the pain he inflicted went well beyond what a fist could ever do.

If only Cole could see that he was nothing like that man.

Cole defended us, kept us safe, protected Mya and me.

Most of the time, he only needed to use his size and the art of intimidation; he preferred it that way. Because beneath that rough exterior of his, beneath those gargantuan muscles and that deep, booming voice, Cole had a heart of gold. I wouldn't have called him a teddy bear, but he certainly came close.

And I knew he would calm down eventually. All I had to do in these outbursts, when he couldn't see past the storm raging inside, was sit back and wait, give him space until it died down a bit. Then, and only then, I could try to reach inside, help him find his reasoning, his sanity, his truth again.

He was almost there.

"I'm so sick of just surviving," Cole yelled, swiping the air with his fist. "I fucking hate him. I could kill him for everything he's done, crack his fucking skull with my bare hands." He held up clenched fists, squeezing as if our father's head really were in his hands. "Instead, we keep running, keep letting him push us around, just like he's always done. We're his little puppets and he's the fucking puppet master."

I didn't' say anything, just listened.

"Why didn't you just let me take care of him when I had the chance? We were this close." He held his hand up and pinched his finger and thumb together. "It would have saved us years of running. Years of just barely getting by. Years of worrying about whether or not he'd snatch Mya out of school, come up behind you one day and just yank her out of your arms. We didn't have to live like this."

He started to cry angry, frustrated tears. A symptom of the years of hell we'd gone through—the death of our mother, years of abuse and neglect, the constant stress and worry since leaving. But those tears were a good thing; they were bringing him back to reality.

"I would have spent the rest of my life in prison, just to not have to worry about you and Mya. If he . . . fuck, if he ever . . . if he . . . " Cole's hands went to his face, smeared his features as he ran them over his cheeks and eyes. "It probably would have just been juvie until I turned eighteen. You know that, Willow."

"I do," I said, quietly. "But could you have really lived with yourself after taking a man's life?"

"He's not a man."

I nodded and took a couple of slow, tentative steps in his direction. "You're right. But it's still a life. I know you, Cole. The guilt . . . you never would have been the same. You wouldn't be who you are today." I rested my hand on his clenched fist, hoping the touch would help ground him again. "You're a good man, Cole. The best. And I couldn't imagine not having you with us, having to visit you behind bars. It would have killed your spirit, everything good in you. This is the lesser of the two evils."

Cole choked back a pained sob. "Why won't he just die already? Piece of shit alcoholic should have killed his kidneys by now. Had a heart attack. Fuck, something!"

I squeezed his hand. "I know."

He held my gaze for a moment, conveying his unspoken grief—the real reason behind his melt down, something neither of us would say out loud—before dropping his furrowed features to the ground at his feet. "Sorry," he mumbled, digging at the dirt with the toe of his boot. "The last thing we need right now is me losing my shit."

"Yeah, you're right, but we deal with some seriously heavy stuff," I said. "I'd think there was something wrong with you if you didn't lose it from time to time."

Cole lifted his head and gave me a smile—a weak one, but a smile, nonetheless. Maybe that meant his temporary loss of sanity had nothing to do with the thoughts running through my own head. Maybe we hadn't been on the same page. Or maybe that smile meant nothing at all.

I only knew that, with this being Winnie's third consecutive breakdown, things were about to get worse . . . much, much worse. For all of us.

***

Just a few feet from the rig, I held up my cardboard sign

that read "Need to get home. Please help." So far, I'd pulled in a little more than a hundred dollars. If we were in Phoenix or Mesa—anywhere but Flagstaff—I probably would have done better. But this tiny little mountain town didn't seem to have much in it, other than the fellow travelers passing through.

Here and there, a few would drop some cash, but most of them just kept on driving past, not even offering a second glance. Maybe it was time to bust out Plan B: applying for an actual job and staying for a while.

Just as that thought ran through my head, a silver Miata pulled up next to me. The driver, a rather handsome man with honey-colored hair and rich brown eyes, rolled down his window, then thrust out a hand containing two one hundred dollar bills. My mouth practically salivated as I took the few steps necessary to grab the cash. But just as my fingers grazed the crisp, green bills and the "thank you" left my mouth, he pulled his hand back.

"Uh-uh-uhh," he said, his lips curling into a snake-like grin that revealed a set of perfect white teeth. "A pretty girl like you should know that nothing in life comes for free."

"Fuck off," I spat, backing away from the car, heading back to my post. That couple hundred dollars could get us the hell out of there, but what he wanted wasn't for sale. My body. My rules. And I'd be damned if some complete stranger with a god complex was going to put his hands (or any other appendage) on it.

"Now, now, that's no way to talk to a gentleman offering

you money." With that sickening smile still plastered on his face, he bent his arm at the elbow, rested it on the open window, and leaned in my direction. "All I'm asking for is a few minutes of your time, and maybe a little bit of that dirty mouth of yours, and you're free to go. A couple hundred dollars richer, I might add."

When I responded with a roll of my eyes, he ducked back into his car.

Good, he's leaving, I thought.

But instead of pulling away, he turned back to me and extended his hand again. He'd added a couple more large bills to the prize. "Look, I'll even up the ante," he said, waving the wad of cash at me. "And I promise, it won't take long. Fifteen minutes, tops."

"You know, I don't make a habit of leveling with assholes like yourself—" I paused for effect. "But apparently you're too dense to take a hint. I'm not selling what you're buying, and I can't go anywhere. I've got six kids back in that rig." I nodded in Winnie's direction." They need their momma. So, either you're going to give me the cash and help us out, or you'll drive on and find some chick who's offering what you're looking for."

When he still didn't move, just sat there glaring at me, I shoved a shaky hand into my pocket and pulled out my cell phone. "Of course, the other option is I can call the cops and have you arrested for harassment and attempting to engage in prostitution which, in case you didn't know, is illegal."

That got him moving.

As he threw his car into drive, he muttered, "Fucking crazy bitch." He squealed out of the parking lot, leaving behind a cloud of dust and burnt-rubber as he headed for the off-ramp. Within seconds, his tail-lights had disappeared.

Thank the gods!

Tough as nails act aside, I'd been scared shitless. All it would have taken . . . what he could have done . . .

Fuck, men were assholes.

I'd learned that from the very first man in my life, the very man who had been put on this earth to protect me and take care of me. Why the hell would some stranger dressed in a monkey suit, offering me money for sex as he leered at me like a walking vagina, treat me any differently?

He wouldn't.

At least Josh served as proof that not all men were jerks. I just wished my wings, which were starting to wither from lack of use, hadn't been too dirty for him. I'd have flown away to find solace and comfort in his arms, right that very second.

But I couldn't.

And I wouldn't.

Because if he'd known from the start who I really was, if he'd seen the horns where he imagined a halo and the charcoal hue of my feathers, he never would have even given me a chance. And I never would have had the chance to imagine that maybe, in a different life or some alternate universe, I could have been something—someone—different.

Happy.

Kate Givans

Beautiful.
Worthy.

Chapter Eight
The Past

Exhausted and just plain burnt out, I plopped down onto the couch. I rolled my eyes to the other end, where the remote sat, and thought about picking it up, maybe watching an episode of *That 70's Show* or catching a movie on Lifetime. But even just reaching that far seemed like an impossible feat.

I had become an expert at managing the household. Grocery shopping, caring for Mya, getting Cole and me off to school, cooking, cleaning, taking care of momma. But between all of that and homework, I was exhausted.

At least dad was home to help now.

He'd just finished his last route, and it was a good thing. Momma hadn't been out of the bedroom in weeks, couldn't even get up to use the bathroom on her own anymore. I couldn't have kept it all together on my own much longer.

But there was still this apprehension about having my dad around. I couldn't really explain it, and I had no idea where it came from, but I was pretty sure it had something to do with the way he looked at me. It made me feel all weird inside, made my guts twist and writhe around like they'd become impossibly tangled shoe strings and he was the one pulling on the ends.

It was weird.

Just like that, like he'd somehow known that I'd been

thinking of him, dad walked through the front door, back from a trip to the store. "Hey there, red," he said, grinning at me as he lifted a brown paper bag to his lips. "Where's your momma?"

"Uh, in bed," I said, unable to avoid thinking about how silly of a question that had been.

"Good. She needs her rest." He lifted the paper bag again, this time wiping his mouth after he took a drink of whatever was inside. "And Cole? Mya? You get them off to bed?"

There was that look again. The one that made me feel sick inside. "Yeah." I gave the clock on the wall a nervous glance as my dad stood there in the doorway, still staring at me. "Well, um, I should go to bed," I said, the words coming out rushed. "School tomorrow."

"Well, now, hold on there." Dad took the few steps necessary to make it over to the couch and then sat down next to me. "I just wanted to tell you how proud I am of you. You been real good at keepin' it all together 'round here."

I wanted to take pride in that compliment, wanted to bask in the well-deserved praise for all the hard work I'd put in over the last few months. But that gnawing feeling inside only got worse. "Thanks," I muttered, looking down at my hands, which twisted and moved of their own free will. I couldn't have stopped them if I tried.

"But, you know, it's important that a girl your age do normal things. Go to the mall, the movies, go shoppin'." He was nodding, more to himself than me, I think. His green eyes looked glassy, distant, as he continued nodding in silence for a beat. "Anyway," he finally said, pausing to take another drink. "You should go spend some time with your friends tomorrow. And here—" Dad leaned forward and reached in his back pocket, producing his wallet after a clumsy moment of almost falling forward onto the floor. "Take some money with you. Get yerself something nice. I know you're 'bout that age to start thinking of buying, er, intimates . . . I won't take you, and your momma can't, but your friends might have an idea of what to get."

His elbow grazed my breast as he fumbled to pull the money from his wallet. *An accident*, I thought to myself as I leaned to the left to give him more room, but the bile rising up in the back of my throat said otherwise.

Finally, he wiggled the bills free and held them out for me. His hand rested so close to my knee, I could feel the heat coming from it, like pins and needles shooting from his skin to mine. I took the money with shaky fingers. My throat was so closed up, my breathing so erratic, I couldn't even mutter a thanks before slowly, numbly lifting myself from the couch to head off to my bedroom.

"And Willow?"

I stopped, just at the end of the living room, right before the hallway, and turned to face my father again.

"Don't go to one of those cheap stores. I mean it, get yerself something nice. Go to that one store, the one where the girls on television are always showing off their braziers."

I nodded, unsure of why it mattered what store I went to.

"I'm sure, even if your friends can't help, they'll know what you need."

And that was that.

But, as I curled up in my bed that night, something felt off. And I could have sworn that, when I woke up in the middle of the night to check on Mya, I'd felt someone watching me, standing in the doorway of my room. When I rolled over in bed to look, there wasn't anyone there, but I just couldn't shake the feeling, not even after giving Mya her bottle and settling back in bed.

And, because of it, I barely slept at all the rest of the night.

The next day, after getting out of school, I walked Cole home. When I checked in on Mya, dad sent me away, reminding me that I needed to spend some time doing "normal girl things." Problem was, I didn't really have any friends.

Not anymore.

So I went to the Walmart nearby. I knew dad had said to go to the mall, but I just didn't have it in me to walk around, spending hours looking at stuff that I couldn't afford and didn't really care about. I also didn't feel like being the butt of any mean girl jokes that day.

I just wanted to go home and sleep.

And so I bought a plain white cotton sports bra. I managed to have enough left over to buy a new package of underwear, some socks, a Ninja Turtles toy for Cole, and a onsie outfit for Mya. All in all, I'd say a pretty good way to spend the money my dad had given me. Momma would be proud.

Only, when I walked through the front door and set my bag down on the couch so I could make myself a sandwich, I got a very different impression from my dad. In fact, he was downright livid as he searched through the bag.

"I thought I told you to go and get something nice!" He waved the cotton bra and package of plain women's briefs at me. "This isn't what I told you to get."

"I—I—I'm sorry," I stuttered, looking down at the floor, mortified that my father had my bra and underwear in his hand. "I just thought . . . with you not working . . . and everything Cole and Mya are missing with mom sick, it might be nice to get them something, too."

"I didn't ask you to get anything for them," he yelled, shoving the items back in the bag and then throwing it, and its contents, across the room. It landed in the corner with a thud and a ruffle of plastic. "I told you to get something nice for *you!* You're the woman of the house now. You're taking care of everyone, cooking and such. I wanted you to get something pretty for yerself."

I whimpered in pain as he grabbed a hold of my wrist, squeezing as he pulled me so close, I could feel the heat of his breath against my face.

"I'm gonna teach you—

"Amos!" My mother's voice cut him off.

I turned abruptly at the sound, and my father lifted his gaze. My mother's thin, frail frame leaned against the walls of the paneled hallway.

Dad didn't miss a beat. "Janine, shouldn't you be in bed?" he asked, releasing my wrist and taking a step back, but still too close for comfort.

"I would be, but . . . " Momma paused, looked at me, and then my hands, which were rubbing the stinging of my wrist, before directing a narrowed set of eyes at my father. "Willow, why don't you take your sister outside to play for a bit? Your father and I need to talk."

"She don't need to go nowhere," dad said, his shoulders lifting, spine straightening as he crossed his arms over his chest. "If she's grown up enough to cause an argument and drag you outta bed, she's grown enough to sit here and listen to whatever comes after."

I looked at my father, and then back at my mother again, afraid I would make the wrong choice. Did I listen to my mother, the sick woman who really should have been in bed but had come out to my defense? Or my dad, the one that I had to deal with, day in and day out, the one I would have to live with once my mother was gone?

"Willow, go on," momma said, a soft smile painting her lips but not coming anywhere close to meeting her eyes, eyes that held the same deep sadness I remembered from the day she'd told me about Mya. "I've got this, honey. Your brother is already out there and your sister is probably awake by now."

I slid past my dad, acutely aware of the angry energy buzzing off of him, and then made my way toward the hallway. Every step seemed like a mile, and something in me felt like it might crack at any second.

When I passed momma, I wanted nothing more than to throw myself into her arms, sob, and let her run her fingers through my hair. But if I did that, I knew she'd probably fall over. So, instead, I settled for her touching my shoulder and then made my way back to Mya's room.

With my baby sister in tow, I headed outdoors, out into the field, where the dandelions were just starting to bloom again. We stayed far enough from the house so that I didn't have to hear the yelling that had started the second I closed the door.

As Mya crawled around in the grass, I started a dandelion chain. Carefully threading each stem through the one before it, I thought of the last time momma and I had been out there, when she'd told me of her pregnancy. When I'd recognized something was wrong, but hadn't understood what. Had she known then about the cancer, and if so, why hadn't she told me then? Had it really been nearly a year since all of that had happened?

In so many ways, it felt like it had been forever ago, but in others, it felt like it'd only been a matter of days. I supposed time, and its passing, changed when someone you loved was dying. Maybe a lot of things did.

Chapter Nine
The Present

Three weeks.

That's how long it took us to get back on the road. Too long, in my opinion, but panhandling hadn't pulled much cash. So instead of relying on the kindness of complete strangers, Cole and I had decided to take shit jobs with alternating schedules. It wasn't worth much, but it had been enough to get us out of Flagstaff and back on the road.

Now we had to hurry up and make it to Los Angeles, our final destination. Mya had been out of school the entire time. I felt bad about that, but creating school records, which could be accessed by our father at any given time, were too much of a risk. It'd be like painting a giant arrow to California for him.

And I wanted us to have some time in L.A., wanted us to stay there until school let out for the year. The weather would be perfect for a little while longer, sunshine and moderate temperatures. When summer came and the heat got to be too much, we could head further north. San Francisco, maybe. I'd never been, but had heard from other roadies that its summers were gorgeous . . . well, gorgeous compared to the southern parts of the country.

I hoped they were right.

"Mojave Desert is just up ahead," Cole said, looking up from the map to focus his gaze on the road in front of us.

"Might be a cool stop."

I shook my head. "Cole, you know we can't afford anymore stops. And with us just fixing the radiator, I'd like to get Winnie out of the heat as soon as possible. She needs some rest, ya know?"

Cole stared out the windshield for a while, the wheels turning in his head. He was thinking about it, I knew it.

"It's not time, Willow," he finally said, setting his jaw, his blue eyes turning to cold, hard stone. "I'm not leaving yet, not until I know you and Mya are going to be okay."

"Cole . . . "

"Damn it, Willow." His voice boomed through the cab as he slammed his fist down on the dash. "I get to decide how my life goes. Wasn't that the whole point? The reason you set this stupid time limit for me? "

"No, Cole!" I yelled, matching his volume and intensity. "That's *not* why we have the agreement. The whole point is for you to have a normal life, one that doesn't involve running, constantly looking over your shoulder. A chance to have a girlfriend, maybe kids, a career."

"Well maybe I don't want those things, Willow. Did you ever think about that? Did you think that maybe, just maybe, keeping you and Mya safe would be more important to me?"

"Yes, Cole." Sadness, pain, and regret replaced the fight in my voice. I swallowed it, forced it to stay at bay while I blinked back the heat of my tears. "And that's exactly why it has to happen, why I made the decision in the first place."

Pissed at me, he lifted himself out of the passenger seat,

shoved his way past me into the back of the rig, and then closed the curtain behind him, shutting me out.

When I heard the familiar creak of the bed in the back, I let my tears loose. I let them run wild and free down my cheeks. I didn't try to wipe them away, even as they blurred my vision. I just let them be what they were: external evidence of the overwhelming ache in my chest.

Seemed my life was full of painful good-byes lately. Josh. Winnie. Cole. I honestly didn't know how much more my heart could take. But I knew, without a doubt, what I would be doing once it came time to leave Los Angeles, the choice I would have to make.

I didn't want to say good-bye to my brother any more than he wanted to leave. But he deserved something more. Something better. And I had decided years ago when that time would be: the day Winnie retired. The old girl wouldn't hold out much longer, and that meant it *was* time.

This would be her last run.

***

I'll have to admit, Los Angeles had been a lot greener than I'd imagined.

I'd been on the west coast before, but not quite this far south. Don't ask me why, but I imagined a ton of sandy beaches and lots of palm trees and concrete. Probably because it was so close to the deserts of Arizona and Nevada. But no, there was grass. And real, honest to goodness trees.

There were palm trees, too, of course, but even in the middle of the city, there seemed to be quite a bit of green.

Maybe it was like Phoenix in that way, folks creating lawns where they didn't belong. But on crack. Or maybe it was just the strangeness of being not quite desert pushed up against the ocean. Either way, I liked it.

Mya did, too.

We spent our days after school going to the beach, browsing the stores, going to the movies. It couldn't have been more different than the Midwest if it tried. And she had adjusted to it rather well—all the extra people and the busyness that came with them, the millions of things to do on the weekends. Her favorite was the Los Angeles Zoo.

Mine was the beach.

Something about listening to the waves crash against the shoreline. Looking out at the horizon and feeling so damn small, like maybe my life, my problems, were nothing more than just a blip on the map. In a way, it made the weeks of missing Josh harder, but in a way, it also helped to ease the constant ache a little.

It reminded me that this time in my life, and all the times that had come before it, were short, fleeting. Despite everything I'd lost, everything I'd given up, I was still so small in the grand scheme of things. My life was just a blip on the map. And it could always be worse. I could have nothing left to fight for. Nothing to live for. I could have all these memories, all this pain, and be completely and utterly alone.

I would be, eventually, but that time was still so far off.

Maybe, by then, I would be okay with it. I could travel to other countries, see the world. Maybe, by some miracle, Josh would still be single and would welcome me with open arms after having some time to heal and finally learning the truth.

Or maybe life would swallow me up and spit me out, deformed and unwanted and I could just slink away into oblivion, non-existence, drift away into a world where hurt and pain and all the people and things you've lost no longer matter.

Maybe I could finally be with my mother, sleep for eternity, let Cole and Mya believe that I'd gone backpacking in Europe or had gone to South America to live in a tree house and spend time living with some indigenous tribe. It wouldn't be too far-fetched for me, and I would have the chance to disappear.

No more nightmares.

No more loss.

No more fear.

No more pain.

A chicken way to go, I know. I'd admonished Josh for that very thing—giving up. But he had so much life left, so much potential. So many opportunities. For him to give up was a waste. Mya and Cole were what I lived for, the only reason I existed, the only reason I had found a way to overcome the horrors of my past. Without them, without Josh . . . I had nothing left.

I was nothing.

So maybe that's the way it was meant to be, dying at the end of a martyr-like life. Maybe it really would be for the best. The gods knew I couldn't take much more, not without unraveling completely; it already felt as if the threads holding me together had become frayed, and no matter how hard I tried, I couldn't seem to make them work anymore, couldn't seem to quite hold it together. Not when the day was perfect, or I had a good day at work, or we managed to catch the latest and greatest movie. Not even when Mya smiled or laughed.

I guess I *could* still be sad and heartbroken with the sun kissing my skin and my toes in the sand. . . if that's what one would even call this—the endless ache, the constant despair, the fear of the future, the numbness that had crept into every part of my life.

I knew these feelings all too well, and I wanted nothing more than to give in to them . . . especially since I knew things weren't going to get better any time soon. But I had to find the strength to hold on and keep fighting, keep moving forward, find a way to stitch up my heart enough that I could finish what I had started. I would do what I needed to for Mya for as long as she needed me.

I had to.

Chapter Ten
The Past

After a while, daddy left in his truck, kicking up dirt and rocks as he sped down the dirt road that led to the highway. I took Mya and Cole inside and set them up with an after-school show so I could make dinner. I had just pulled a box of hamburger helper out of the pantry when something in my peripheral moved.

"Momma!"

Curled up on the floor next to the kitchen island, my mother looked like a broken, beaten child. I rushed to her side, falling to my knees on the floor beside her. I swore I could hear her bones rattling as she shook—from fear or from pain, I wasn't sure. But then, gods, then she lifted her head and looked up at me. One side of her face was red—bright, blood red—and swollen to twice its normal size. I'd never seen anything quite like it.

Tears instantly started to run down my cheeks. Tiny gasps of air quickly turned to sobs. "Oh, momma. I—I'm so—so sorry. Th—this is m—my fault. I—I—"

Even through what had to be the most unimaginable pain, my mother smiled. "Oh, sweetheart, you didn't do this," she said, pulling strands of hair from my salty, tear-streaked cheeks.

I shook my head and extended a shaky hand toward her face. My fingers stopped just short of what I could already tell would be a deep, dark bruise. It's a wonder the bones in her face hadn't shattered.

I couldn't believe my father had done this to her. For what? For standing up for me? For stopping him from . . . what had he been ready to do when momma stepped in the middle of his yelling and screaming? When he'd wrapped his hand so tightly around my wrist it made me cry out in pain, made me want to curl into a little ball and hide? Left a red mark on my arm almost identical to the one on momma's . . .

And just like that, everything started to come together.

All the "accidents" over the years seemed to coincide with daddy being home. With his off-days on his routes. The bruises. The days of momma limping around, the random pains in her side, back, shoulders. He'd been hitting her, hurting her, all that time.

I knew they'd fought a lot, and could recall many nights where I'd cried in bed, listening to him scream and yell, the clatter of things being thrown around the house, my momma's cries. I'd been too young to really put it all together at the time.

Or maybe I just hadn't wanted to.

But right then and there, with momma crumpled on the floor, her battle wounds staring me in the face, I couldn't deny it any longer. My mother, my beautiful, kind, amazing mother, had married a monster. Had three children with him. And would most likely die with him standing next to her.

"Why?" I asked.

That one word held so many different meanings, all at once. Why had she married him? Why had she stayed? Why had she brought children into this destructive relationship? Why would she hide it from us, from me? Why would she leave us now, with him, with the horrible person she'd chosen to dedicate her entire life to?

After studying my face for the longest time, momma finally spoke. "Willow, honey, help me to bed, please," she said, extending her hand, apparently refusing to give me answers. Or maybe there weren't any answers to give. Maybe now, at the end of her life, she wondered the very same things herself. Or maybe she was just too tired and in too much pain. Maybe she would tell me later, give me the answers I suddenly needed as badly as I needed air to breathe.

Rather than grill her, or push her, I took her hand and went to pull, but then stopped, realizing that I might end up hurting her more that way. So, instead, I stood, bent over and placed my hands beneath her armpits, lifting as I stood upright again.

Once I had momma back in bed, tucked beneath her covers, I went to leave and finish making dinner for Cole and Mya. But just as I turned to go, momma reached out and grabbed a hold of my wrist—not hard like daddy had done, but enough to get my attention.

"Willow, listen to me," she said, eyes wide and wild when I turned to face her.

I wasn't sure whether to feel angry, disgusted, or sorry

for her. I suppose I felt a little of all three, and maybe more. But then, as she started to speak, all of that faded away and became something deeper, more primal, something born of a need for survival and self-preservation: cold, hard, bone-chilling fear.

"You keep your sister and brother safe, you hear me?" she said, speaking so soft and so fast that I had to lean in closer and strain my ears to hear. "There's a receipt in my purse, and on the back, there's a phone number and the word Vee, spelled with two e's. You call that number, and don't let your daddy know. Make sure he's not around. Make sure no one is around, you hear? You call it and you do exactly as you're told."

"W—what's the number for?" I asked, my shaky voice barely able to force the words out.

"Just do as you're told, Willow. Understand? Can you do that for me?"

Unable to even speak anymore, I just nodded.

"Good. Now . . . " Momma pulled the covers up to her chin and then smiled softly, as if we hadn't just had the single most frightening conversation ever. "Let me rest. I—I'm feeling a little sleepy."

I wanted to stay. I had so many questions, and felt like so much had gone unsaid . . . but she'd already fallen asleep by the time I figured out how to make my mouth work again. And so, instead of waking her, I tiptoed out of the room and closed the door behind me.

Chapter Eleven
The Present

My eyelids fluttered shut as Josh's soft, warm lips trailed across the swell of my breasts, down my sides and along my hip bones. I knew what came next. I also knew this wasn't real; it was only a dream, but I certainly didn't want anyone to wake me.

Not when his mouth had enveloped the folds of my sex and the gentle lapping of his tongue had me whimpering already. In a matter of seconds—entirely too soon, even for a dream—my body had started to coil and tense, begging for the release that only he could give me, a release that no one else had ever granted. I craved it, needed it, more than I'd ever needed anything.

When it first came, it felt like an explosion, and then I felt like I'd been catapulted into the air. I plummeted in a spiral, speeding for the ground, but then, at the last second, my wings took flight and I found myself floating on a cloud above the world. Nothing could touch me, not my past, not the constant fight for survival, not the pressures of being the protector for my siblings. Even the uncertainty of our futures fell away up there on my cloud.

I wanted to live there forever.

But as his body crept up mine and my eyes fluttered back open, I found myself quite far from my beautiful, fluffy cloud. I was in the depths of hell, staring into the eyes of the devil himself. The scent of cheap whiskey and rotting flesh from his gums cut off my air supply. The rough calluses of his fingers made me cringe as he grasped my hips. The red, hot pain, paired with the deep-seeded disgust as he thrust into me, made me retch. Tears flowed down the sides of my face, but I knew they would be useless; they couldn't evoke any kind of compassion or gentleness inside the beast.

Because this wasn't some fairytale.

He wasn't capable of those kinds of emotions. Never had been, never would be. He was only capable of anger, hatred, malice, hurt. And he would deliver all of that, and more, until the day I died, if not through real life, then at least through my nightmares—nightmares that had all but disappeared when I'd been nestled in Josh's arms. With him gone, they'd returned full force, only worse. They had morphed into some sick, twisted game, used my memories of him and tainted them, turned them into something ugly.

Sick.

Horrible.

Inhumane.

Just like the man responsible for them in the first place.

Chapter Twelve
The Past

I lay in bed, staring up at the ceiling, unable to sleep. No matter how hard I tried, I couldn't stop thinking of what momma had said, the fear in her eyes, the terror in her voice. Would daddy really hurt me or Cole or Mya? Were we in danger? Who would be at the other end of the line if I called that number? What would happen to us?

So many questions, and no answers.

Frustrated and angry, but mostly afraid, I punched my pillow in an attempt to make it more comfortable and then rolled over onto my side, facing away from my door. That's when I noticed the shadow on my wall.

Surrounded by light coming from the hallway, the figure swayed like some ghostly being, side to side and then shrinking and growing. At first, I thought it might be momma, but that couldn't be right. She would have just come and sat down on the end of my bed if she wanted to talk to me. Then, when the figure on my wall lifted something to his lips, I knew for certain who it was, standing there in my doorway, watching me while I slept.

Something screamed inside my head—not a word, exactly, but a feeling. A sickening one that sucked the air out of my lungs and sent shivers down my spine. Fear had apparently dropped the thermostat in my room down to below freezing, and I swore the thundering of my heartbeat had started echoing off the walls.

I don't know why I was so scared, other than my mother's strange behavior—that and the horrible dark bruise that I knew would cover most of her face the next morning. But that wasn't the reason. This was . . . different somehow. And, as the figure left my doorway, its size growing on my wall as it came nearer, the sickening dread in the pit of my stomach turned my intestines to concrete and filled my veins with lead.

He was coming for me.

I didn't know why.

I didn't know what to do.

I could only try to focus on slowing my breath, stopping the short gasps that were coming harder and faster with each and every footfall of my father's approaching form. The tightening of my entire body as he sat down at the foot of my bed. The gagging that began as soon as I caught my first whiff of whiskey. The scream ready to erupt from my throat as his hand fell on the blanket right behind me, despite how the pull of them seemed to cut off my airway.

But all of that was nothing compared to the way my entire body froze, like it'd been set in ice, when his hand reached around my body, first touching my stomach and then moving upward toward my throat.

He was going to choke me, murder me in my sleep.

I was certain of it.

Until his hand stopped at what little bit of cleavage I had.

The blanket and the t-shirt I slept in were still between my breast and his hand, but they did nothing to dampen the violation. They didn't stop the need to vomit. They didn't stop the tears from flowing down my cheeks as he squeezed my flesh in his hands, over and over, as if my breast was some sort of stress ball.

He grunted. "Yer fillin' out real nice," he slurred in a low, deep voice. "Might even have better tits than yer momma."

I whimpered, despite my attempts to hold it in.

"Shhh . . . now, don't worry. You're going to like this. It might hurt a bit at first, but it'll feel good real soon. I promise."

My whimpers gave way to a deep, heavy sob when he began to pull the covers away from me. I clenched them in my fists, holding onto them for dear life.

"You can scream alls you want, but ain't nobody going to save you," he said, letting go of the blanket to grasp my face in his hand. My jaw ached as he dug his fingers in and forced me to look at him. "In fact, I might like it if you scream and fight me. Makes it more fun."

His eyes gleamed in the little bit of light filtering in my room, but it did nothing to balance out the maniacal twist of his face, the ugliness of his blackened teeth, the stench of body odor and whiskey mingling together to create a perfume that singed the inside of my nose and paralyzed the rest of me.

The next twenty minutes of my life were the worst I'd ever experienced up to that point. Each second seemed like an hour. Each rough touch of his hands felt like razorblades ripping at my skin. The penetration of his fingers, and eventually his penis, ripped me from the inside out and, though the burning sensation of my female parts did eventually subside, the deeper parts of me—my heart, my spirit, my soul—would never be the same. They'd been shredded, mauled, tossed in a blender and then poured back into me, useless and now incapable of filling up the spaces they were meant to occupy.

As he left my room, left me stripped naked and in a fit of sobs, he told me I was officially a woman now. "Woman of the house," he said.

Funny how I'd always thought that my transition from girl to woman would be something different—gradual, special . . . beautiful even, like the breaking of a butterfly from its cocoon.

Apparently, I'd been wrong.

Chapter Thirteen
The Present

"Where are you going?" Cole asked as I trudged down the pavement, away from Winnie.

I turned and walked backwards for a few steps and lifted my elbow further up into the air. The movement caused the green canvas bag hanging over my shoulder to shift. "To do laundry," I said before turning back around.

"That's not how this works, Willow!" Cole yelled from Winnie's drop-down steps. "You can't just leave and not tell me where you're going."

"I just did," I yelled back, not even bothering to turn around this time.

I didn't even cringe when I heard the door slam shut.

He had been angry with me for weeks, and it was only about to get worse. But I didn't care. Not anymore. Well . . . I did, actually, but I had to convince myself that I didn't. If I let myself contemplate the next couple of weeks, what was to come, I wouldn't follow through.

And I wouldn't be able to live with myself if I backed out; this was too important.

So, instead of thinking about it, I just went through the motions. I hid away Cole's money, kept it separate from what Mya and I would need. I pushed at him, prodded his little anger button, forcing him to either leave on his own accord or, at the very least, be grateful that I'd left him behind.

I needed him to not come after us.

I wanted him to move on and live.

But it was a process that took careful planning and preparation. One that took every ounce of will I possessed, tore me open and bled me dry, made me weak and vulnerable, which was exactly why I had to take these moments to breathe. Moments of solidarity to reflect and remind myself of why I was doing it in the first place, why it had to be this way.

Doing laundry wasn't exactly the type of reflection I'd wanted, but it was the best I could get at the moment. I'd searched the area for bridges or cliffs, somewhere I could find a bit of release, but so far hadn't come up with anything where people wouldn't see me. I didn't need another repeat of Old Mill Road. I wasn't trying to kill myself; just something about being up there, the wind against my skin, the hair whipping at my face . . . it calmed me somehow.

The ocean was the closest thing I'd found, but all the people there—the children laughing, teenagers hanging out with their friends and thinking nothing of the world around them, the families going about their normal, happy lives— made it impossible to find clarity.

So washing and folding laundry would just have to do.

The Karina Halle book tucked in my laundry bag couldn't hurt either. I sighed, thinking how nice it would be if my life were more like one of her books. But then again, I guessed I was a little like Ellie Watts, constantly moving from one life to another, harboring more secrets than a dirty politician. Just replace the drug lord and his thugs with a former truck-driving, sexually, and physically abusive father hell-bent on making you pay and you sort of had my life . . . sort of.

At least Ellie had love, a chance at a future, a life.

All those things I'd never have sucker punched me in the gut as soon as I stepped into the trailer park laundry mat. I'd been there before, but I didn't remember a laundry cart. Yet, today, there it was, taunting me, forcing me to remember my day at the laundry mat with Josh.

I wanted to smile at the thought of him crammed in that little basket, wheeling around, scared enough to piss himself . . . maybe I did and my brain just didn't register it over the ache of missing him that had started spreading through me like a debilitating disease. A disease that left me feeling numb as the laundry bag slid from my fingers and hit the tile floor with a thud, clouded my brain and hid all the risks as I pulled my cell phone from my pocket, searched for his number, and hit send.

"Hello?"

His voice. His perfect, deep, soothing voice ran over me and through me, filling all the aching pieces inside if me, making me whole again, if only for a few short seconds.

"Willow?"

The ache and brokenness of my name coming through the line shattered me into a million little pieces, proved just how much I'd hurt him. I opened my mouth to speak, thought of all the things I could say to try and ease his pain—

that it wasn't him, that I wasn't worth it, and he should live and love someone else, move on, be happy. Then it hit me . . . he knew it was me, and I'd just broken rule number two.

Panic sent the phone flying from my hands. It clattered to the ground and landed beneath the folding table. Tears burned my eyes as my body slid down the exterior of one of the wall dryers. I sat on the ground, shaking, crying, an empty shell full of nothing but regret and pain and fear.

What had I done?

Gods, what had I done?

Chapter Fourteen
The Past

"Hello?" The voice on the other end of the line sounded soft and kind . . .

But it didn't make me any less afraid.

"Um . . . my—my momma told me to call you." I twisted the phone cord around my finger as I spoke to the mystery voice on the other end of the line, the owner of the number from my mother's purse.

A gasp came through the receiver. "Willow? Willow, is that you?"

Something about her knowing my name frightened and calmed me, all at the same time. How that was possible, I didn't know. I only knew that my hands had gone numb and my throat had gone impossibly dry.

I couldn't do this.

Seconds after I placed the phone back on the cradle, it rang again, echoed through the house like a fire alarm. I must have jumped five feet in the air before snatching it up and slamming it back down again.

I didn't know who that woman was, but I couldn't tell her everything that had happened. I couldn't tell her that my mother was dead, that she'd fallen asleep the very same night that the remainder of my innocence had been ripped from me. That I suspected my father had killed her, either in her sleep, or from the blow to her head just hours before.

Of course he'd covered that up well, had told the morgue that she'd fallen trying to get out of bed and that the fall must have been what killed her. And he managed to cry the tears of a grief-stricken husband, a man left to raise his children alone.

But raising us was the furthest thing from his mind.

I hadn't been to school in weeks because, every night, after throwing his smelly, sweaty body on top of me, he would leave. Morning would come and we'd still be home alone. I couldn't leave Mya, so I would send Cole off to the bus stop and call myself in sick.

How much longer I could do that, I didn't know.

Add that to a long list of other things that didn't make sense, things that had my twelve-year-old self lost, confused, and empty, and beneath that, dirty. Disgusting. And no matter how many times I showered, how hard and long I scrubbed my body with soap, the feeling just wouldn't go away. Like somehow, the filth had settled itself into my bones and become a permanent part of me.

Was this what it felt like to be a woman?

Or had I just gone crazy?

***

I had just put Mya down for her nap and was making myself a peanut butter and jelly sandwich when a knock came at the front door. The sudden break in silence startled me and the butter knife fell from my hand, hitting the ground in an ear-shattering clang. I stared at it, as though maybe it could tell me whether or not I should check to see who might be standing outside our home.

The droves of visitors bearing casseroles and flowers and offers to baby-sit had died down quite some time ago, about two weeks after my mother's death. Could the person behind the door be a straggler? Had they been trapped under a rock and maybe not heard of my mother's death until now?

There was only one way to find out.

I quietly crept to the living room and peeked through the window, being careful not to let the curtains ruffle as I pulled them out just enough that I could see the front door. On the front step, a tall woman with silver hair looked up, as if she were analyzing the condition of our home. Her suit dress moved with her as she took a step back. My heart thudded noisily against my rib cage as I watched her look right, down toward the driveway, and then left, in my direction. I held my breath, certain she would see me, but after a few moments, she stepped forward and knocked again.

I released my breath, slow and even, so as not to make too much noise. Maybe if she couldn't hear me, couldn't see me, she'd leave. I didn't know who she was, or why she was there, but something told me that I shouldn't answer the door, that her being there somehow meant trouble for me. Or maybe it was just paranoia because school was still in session, and that's where I should have been, not home, alone, caring for my baby sister. Either way, I knew I had to get away from the window before she spotted me.

I slinked back into the kitchen and slid myself down to the floor against the kitchen island. I didn't breathe until I heard an engine turning and the crunch of tires traveling down the gravel road had faded.

Chapter Fifteen
The Present

Friday nights were hell, not just because of the long hours or how busy we were, but because, by the end of the night, I'd feel drained from flirting with drunk and sometimes handsy men, and all for the sake of snagging the best tip possible. It didn't make me many friends among the other female servers, but I didn't much give a shit.

They flaunted their asses just as much as I did, sometimes more. Sometimes they did things I wouldn't do, like sitting on the laps of horny, self-entitled pricks who believed women had been placed on this planet to please them. Some would even go home with the regulars, just to increase their weekly earning potential.

Not me.

Not ever.

Not for anyone.

And that included the dark haired professor-looking guy on the other side of the counter who just so happened to be throwing back his seventh rum and Coke. "Hey, sweet lips, can I get another one of these?" he slurred, leaning up over the bar to get a little closer to me as I poured a beer from the tap.

"Sure thing, sugar," I threw over my shoulder. "Just give me a sec, okay? And, for gods' sake, sit down before you fall on your damn head. My boss'll kill me if I have to close the bar down to get an ambulance in here for your drunk ass."

"Just trying to get a better look at yours," he said, grinning.

I turned my back to him and rolled my eyes as I finished filling the mug in my hand. Some men had no shame. No shame at all.

After setting the tap down on the counter for another customer, I went to pour professor guy his drink. "This is your last one for the night," I told him, placing the glass down on the napkin in front of him.

"Aw, you're cutting me off?" he asked, head tilted to the side as he gave me his best fake and very drunken pout.

"I am. And, unless you have a ride home, I'm calling you a cab, too."

"Well, if you're going to cut me off, I guess I can't stall anymore." His dark brown eyes glinted with mischief as his goofy grin grew, taking up most of his pretentious face. "I was really hoping to get your number. Maybe take you out sometime. Show you a good time."

"Awe, honey, I'd love to," I said, my voice dripping with false sweetness, hopefully masking my desire to throw out some sarcastic remark. "But my boyfriend's here, and if he sees me giving you my number . . . well, let's just say he's the jealous type. But, if he weren't here, I'd totally give you my number."

"Oh, yeah? And where's this boyfriend of yours?" Mr. Suave asked. His perfect, white teeth disappeared as he narrowed his eyes slightly. Apparently, he wasn't buying the line of bullshit I was trying to sell.

I lifted my head to scan the crowd for the biggest, bulkiest guy in the room. "He's right over . . . " My words trailed off as my gaze landed on someone familiar, someone I would have recognized anywhere. "I'll—uh—I'll be right back," I said, sliding around the counter in a complete haze, making my way to the figure standing in the back on weak, shaky legs.

It couldn't be him, could it?

It didn't make any sense.

Yet, the closer I got, the more confident I became that it had to be him. Just had to be. No one else stood with that same slight air of confidence, not without looking arrogant. No one else wore a J. Crew hoodie quite like him, with shoulders just defined enough that it fit snug at the top and gave away just a hint of what might be underneath. And not a single ass on this planet could fill a pair of jeans quite like his.

His name floated from my lips, sounding more like a strangled cry than words, as I stepped up behind him. When he didn't turn around, I reached out to touch him on the shoulder. He turned to face me just before my fingers made contact.

"Oh!" I cried out in shock when a pair of sapphire eyes met mine instead of the brown ones I'd expected. I immediately stepped backwards, bumping into a table. "I— I'm sorry. I, uh, I thought you were someone else." I gripped the table for support and then whirled around, turning away from him in an attempt to hide the flush heating my face as the man who clearly wasn't Josh laughed.

"It's okay," he said, stepping up beside me before I could flee. His mouth came so dangerously close to my ear, I could feel the heat of his breath, smell the whiskey as he spoke. "I get that a lot. But since your friend isn't here, maybe I could buy you a drink instead."

"I—I'm sorry," I said, again, shaking my head, flinching away, trying like hell to find an escape route, a break in the crowd.

"Are you all right?" the Josh poser asked, touching my elbow. "You look—"

I didn't hear the rest because I'd already started screaming. "Don't touch me! Don't fucking touch me!" My hands met his chest in an angry, defensive, but useless shove. "Get away!"

"Whoa! Hey! He brought his hands up and stepped back, retreating into his group of buddies. "I didn't mean anything by it."

I heard him mutter something like, "Crazy bitch" as I took off into the crowd. Everything seemed so loud, so chaotic, as I made my way to the door. And every person I bumped into smelled of whiskey and sweat.

I had to get out. I needed air. Space. Sanity.

But as I flew through the door, out into the salty air, I wondered if sanity even existed for me anymore. First a phone call that I never should have made, and then hallucinating, seeing Josh in places that he clearly wasn't?

Had I finally gone mad?

***

By the time I made it to the trailer and put the car in park, my body felt completely deflated. I had every intention of heading inside, going straight to the bedroom. All I wanted was to put on my pajamas, take some Ambien, and go to bed. But apparently I'd wandered into the Twilight Zone because that was the night that just wouldn't die.

Cole sat at the dinette, arms crossed over his chest, eyes trained on me the second I walked inside. "We need to talk," he said.

I groaned and brought my hand to my forehead. "Is it something that can wait?" I asked, jamming my thumb into my temple and squeezing in an attempt to stave off my impending headache. "I had the worst night ever, and I could really use some sleep before my shift with Mya tomorrow."

"No, it can't."

My brow lifted at his tone, the hardness of it, the way it demanded my full attention. "Okaaaay . . . " I slumped down in the seat across from him, studied the hard set of his jaw, his tight, thinned lips, the bob of his Adam's apple as he cleared his throat.

Oh, shit. This was it.

Cole was leaving.

I wanted to cry, beg him to stay, but I knew this day would come. Hell, I'd pushed it for weeks, just so I wouldn't have to do it myself. Better for him to go on his own, leave willingly, than for me to cut the ties and potentially damage everything we'd built over the years.

But that didn't mean I wanted him to go.

"Willow . . . I—I think you should talk to someone," Cole said, finally speaking, looking down at his clasped hands resting on the table, refusing to make eye contact.

"Talk to someone?" I asked, apprehension kicking my heart into overdrive.

"You . . . " Cole paused and cleared his throat. "The nightmares. Willow, they're bad. I—I can hear you screaming every single night. They haven't been this bad since . . ." He cleared his throat again and closed his eyes. His lips disappeared and his nostrils flared as he took a deep breath before opening his eyes and lifting his gaze to mine. "I'm worried. You're all over the place. Lani just called, said you took off out of the bar after freaking out on a customer. And you've been pushing me away for weeks. I—I don't know what to think, except that maybe it's time to think about doing something different. Maybe finally finding a way to gain custody of Mya. Putting that piece of shit behind bars before everything falls apart, before we lose her."

I must have sat there in complete shock for a good five minutes before finally forming a coherent thought. "Cole, we've talked about this. We can't go to anyone. I could be charged with kidnapping. Maybe you, too, now. It's not worth the risk. And I don't need to *talk to someone*. I'm fine."

"No, Willow, you're not." Cole said, shaking his head, his blue eyes filled with so much sadness and pain. "You can't keep going on like this. *I* can't keep going on like this."

My shoulders pulled back. My spine straightened. "You don't have to," I said, lifting my chin, hoping it hid how weak and hallow I felt inside. "It's time anyway. Winnie's done, Cole. It's over. Time for you to move on."

Cole let out a bark of a laugh. "If you think I'm leaving Mya with you right now, when you're like this, you're in more trouble than I thought."

"I'm not—"

He raised his hand to silence me. "Look, I'm grateful for everything you've done for me, Willow. And for Mya. I don't know if any of us would have made it if it weren't for you. But you've given up so much for us. Maybe it's time for you to live your life, find something that makes you happy, create a healthy and normal life for yourself. I'm old enough now to take care of Mya, and I'm on all her records."

Tears burned at the corners of my eyes and immediately broke free, burning my cheeks as they made their way to the table between us. "I—I can't—"

"Yes, you can, Willow. It's okay. You can let go now."

But I couldn't.

I wouldn't.

Not when letting go meant I'd have nothing left to hold onto.

Chapter Sixteen
The Past

Dad came home just a little before Cole. As cabinets in the kitchen opened and slammed shut, I hid in my room with Mya in my lap. I held my breath and kept my hand over her mouth to keep her quiet as his footsteps passed by. She squirmed in my arms, irritated that I was trying to keep her still and quiet, but I didn't release her until I heard the door to his room shut.

I couldn't hide in there much longer. I knew that. Cole would come home soon. I'd have to make dinner, bathe Mya, put both of my siblings to bed, and then wait for him to come to me, just as he did every other night. But for now, I could pretend to be a normal almost teenager, hanging out in my room, listening to the radio with a pair of headphones, studying the school work I'd had Cole pick up for me so I didn't fall too far behind.

That was until it all came crashing down.

My false sense of normalcy, my bubble of safety, shattered with the sound of a car door slamming shut outside. She was back . . . whoever *she* was.

Time stood still when I heard the knock at the door, my father's footsteps making their way back down the hall, the front door opening and then closing, the softness of a woman's voice alternating with my father's deep, jagged one. Minutes, maybe hours passed by and I could still hear them.

And then my bedroom door opened.

My father's frame loomed in the doorway. He was wearing the most uncharacteristic smile in existence; it had to have hurt. But nothing, not even a genuine grin, could have balanced out the darkness in his gaze, the silent warning that I knew existed.

I swallowed hard against the dryness in my throat and nodded, acknowledging the unspoken threat, and then numbly bent over to pick Mya up off the floor. One of the blocks she'd been playing with came with her and went straight to her mouth.

"I'll take her," my father said, extending his hands for her as I approached.

On instinct, I turned my body to pull Mya away from him. My fingers gripped at her waist as I stood there in the doorway, glaring at the monster in front of me. I didn't want him to touch her, let alone hold her. "I'll take her," I clipped, lifting my chin in defiance.

So what if I paid for it later.

My father's jaw tensed as he narrowed his eyes at me, a confirmation that I would, indeed pay later. "Fine," he said, his forced cheerful tone and painful looking smile returning as he stepped back and allowed me to pass through my door.

I could feel him watching me as I made my way down the hallway to the living room, holding Mya on my hip. She babbled and gnawed away at the cloth block, completely oblivious to the way my limbs stiffened with each step, as if somehow bone and flesh were turning to wood. Not even the floral scent of the woman's perfume, which reminded me of my mother, could reach me, relax me, and by the time I sat down on the sofa, facing her as she sat in my father's recliner, even my lungs felt petrified.

"Willow," the woman with laugh lines around her mouth and eyes said, leaning forward just a little, not so much that she invaded my personal space, but enough to convey some sort of intimacy or connection. "I'm Veronica. You called me earlier today?"

"Yes, ma'am," I said, my voice broken and high-pitched from the painful lump growing in my throat.

The edges of her mouth crinkled a little with her soft but sincere smile. "Can I ask why?"

The nodule in my throat grew to the size of a softball, and no matter how hard I tried, I just couldn't force it back down, couldn't find my voice, so I shrugged instead.

"I knew your mother, you know?"

I nodded.

"Did she happen to tell you how or why?"

My brows scrunched together as I shook my head.

"I knew your mother back when she was pregnant with you." Veronica smiled again as she clasped her hands in her lap. "I'm a volunteer for one of the local domestic violence shelters, and that's where your mother and I met. Once she completed the program there, I helped her get into transitional housing—that's a special kind of housing set aside for victims. They can go there after they finish the initial program. She lived there for almost two years before coming back to your father. We stayed in touch for a while, talked about you, mostly. Then Cole came along and . . . well, I suppose caring for two children kept her pretty busy. She called less often, and then just not at all. But I did assure your mother that she could call if she ever needed me . . . and then to hear you on the other end of the line . . . concerned me."

I didn't understand.

My mother lived in a domestic violence shelter? Transitional housing? All of that, only to return to the monster that called himself my father? As much of a risk as it was, talking to this woman, I needed answers.

"Why?"

"Why, what?" Veronica asked, tilting her head to the side a bit. "Why did she come back?"

I nodded.

Veronica's lips pressed together in a tight frown. "You know, it's hard to understand why victims of abuse do the things they do. Why children who are abused still love their parents. Why battered women return to the very man that hurt them, maybe almost killed them. Personally, I think it's a combination of things. I think it's fear, mostly, but also a hope that the person will change. And, as impossible as it sounds, love."

I looked to the hallway, nervous my father might be listening. "I—I don't know how she could," I whispered, leaning forward so Veronica could hear me better, just in case he was eavesdropping on our conversation.

Veronica nodded. "And I'm guessing that's why you called?"

My throat closed up again, reminding me that, while this woman might have known my mother, she posed a risk to my family. I wasn't sure why I felt that way. Shame. Fear. A sense of guilt for the things that my father did to me. And a feeling that, if I could find a way to verbalize it, tell someone the awful truth—Veronica, anyone—my worst fear would be confirmed.

This was my fault.

I'd stopped fighting months ago. I just shut it out and shut it off the best I could. It didn't hurt anymore. I didn't cry when he did it. And I had pretty much given up on washing away the dirt, the filth, the stench that seemed to follow me everywhere. Because it was pretty pointless. So maybe I deserved to stay right where I was. Maybe I deserved my punishment, night after night, week after week, month after month.

"Willow? What is it?" Veronica reached across the space between us, extending her arm to touch my leg.

On instinct, I flinched and pulled my body away. The reason why must have been written all over my face because Veronica's hand immediately went to her lips and her eyes shimmered with tears.

"Oh, God. Willow, honey, what has he done?" she asked, her hand shaking as she continued to hold it to her mouth.

"N—n—nothing," I stuttered, lifting Mya and hugging her close, like she could somehow protect me or ground me

or hide me. "It's just—I don't really know you." It wasn't a lie
. . . exactly.

"Willow, if he's hurt you or your siblings . . . Honey,
there are things—programs, facilities—in place that can help.
They can protect you." She leaned forward again, cupped her
hand to the side of her mouth and whispered the rest. "I can
take you out of here right now. All of you. This very second."

I stared at Veronica, analyzing the validity of her
statement, her sincerity. Could she really save us? Take us
from this place? Put an end to the nightmare that had
become my life? Was I even willing to risk it, knowing what
the consequence would be if she failed to deliver? Didn't I
have to try, if not for myself, then at least for Cole and Mya?

"He—he's—I—" Why couldn't I get the words out?

"It's okay, honey," she said, reaching out for me again
and then pulling her hand back, obviously remembering the
way I'd reacted just moments before. "Just nod if he's hurt
you somehow."

I couldn't.

I couldn't nod because I couldn't breathe past the
burning ache in my chest, the feeling that something had
reached inside, grasped a hold of my lungs, and was
squeezing all the air out of them, sucking the life out of me.

I released Mya and clutched at my chest with hands that
had gone numb. I gasped, over and over. I needed air.
Needed to breathe. Needed my head to stop feeling like it
would explode at any second. Needed my heart to slow down,
to stop pounding so hard I could hear it in my ears,

whooshing, thrumming as it crashed against my rib cage.

"Willow? Willow?"

I tried to look at Veronica again, tried to focus in on her face, to tell her I couldn't breathe, but no matter how hard I tried, I couldn't see her, couldn't find her, couldn't speak. I couldn't control my body anymore.

I thought I felt a hand on my shoulder, but that only made everything worse. I think I might have started screaming, or crying, or maybe I'd curled up in a ball on the floor. I don't' really remember. Everything seemed to be happening in slow motion, yet so fast. The yelling. The shouting. The blinding light from outside rushing in and then disappearing when the front door slammed shut.

But none of it seemed real.

It was like being trapped inside of some place where time and space and everything in between had been altered. As the black spots started to take away my vision, eventually giving way to nothing but darkness, I couldn't help but think that maybe that place—the prison I'd been thrust into and couldn't escape—rested somewhere in my own mind and soul, my own self.

And that only frightened me more.

Because, as bad as things had become, as drastically as my life had changed in just two short years, I'd always had the remnants of my mother—the good things she'd poured into me over the years, that last little bit of her light left inside of me. Without it, I had only the dark, empty remains of a girl that once was and that should have been. I would have said I had nothing, but I still had Mya and Cole. I just didn't know how I could ever protect them when I couldn't even protect myself.

Chapter Seventeen
The Present

I clutched the envelope in my hands to my chest. Maybe I could rip my heart out and place it in there as proof that this wasn't what I wanted to do, that I'd give anything to have our lives play out differently, to create that happily ever after for us all.

But those didn't exist, did they?

And now I had to do what I knew was right, even if it killed me.

With shaky hands, I placed the envelope on the table and then fanned my fingers above it, stalling just a moment longer, afraid to let go and of what awaited me out there in the world.

"I'm going to be late," Mya whined, popping her head inside the trailer, pulling my attention away from the contents of the envelope.

"Coming," I said, choking back the tears, forcing a smile on my face as I turned to face her. Somehow, I managed to hold it together as we walked down the steps, and climbed into the car, but the second the door closed, my face fell. I bit my lip to hold back the sob, but I couldn't stop the tears as I watched Winnie disappear in the rear view mirror.

When we passed the gates to the park and I could no longer see her anymore, I closed my eyes for a moment and gripped the steering wheel until my knuckles ached. "Good-bye, Cole," I said, the words nothing more than a broken breath passing through my lips.

Chapter Eighteen
The Past

Groggy and disoriented, I sat up in a bed that wasn't my own, in a room I didn't recognize. The only source of light in the room—an artificial yellow—came through a set of vinyl blinds drawn over a long, wide window. It cast long shadows along the walls and the furniture, which consisted of nothing more than the bed I was on, a television, a nightstand, and a dresser. A soft hum filled the room, playing like an ominous soundtrack to the last moments I could remember, moments that seemed fuzzy, at best.

I remembered Veronica, the way she pushed and prodded for answers that I just couldn't give, words I couldn't make come, a trust that I couldn't find—not because I didn't want to, but because I don't think it existed inside of me anymore. But that didn't explain how I'd ended up here, in this room, in the dark, alone.

Maybe I'd just fallen asleep, and this was just a strange nightmare, some kind of subconscious metaphor for how alone I felt in my own life, how horribly dark everything that used to be bright had become.

It made sense.

When the door opened and the shadowed demon stepped into the room, I knew immediately who it was. I didn't have to see his face to recognize him. I didn't need to hear his voice. The stagger in his step and the almost sickeningly sweet and tangy scent of whiskey gave him away.

I considered screaming. If this was a dream, then it wouldn't matter, right? I could scream and no one would hear me, not even him. Maybe it would wake me up. But, even in a nightmare, the sight of him paralyzed me, cut off my airway, suffocated me. Because even if it wasn't real, even if it was just a nightmare, he could hurt me, torture me, taunt me, threaten me, remind me of just how dirty and evil I'd become.

What would my mother think of me now? Of the things I'd done, and of the things I knew I would continue to do? Would she look at me with more disgust than the distorted face now looming over mine? Would she nod in approval as my father's rough, calloused hands wrapped around my neck? Would she even shed a tear as I gasped for air, clawed at the fingers flexing tighter and tighter?

"Pull some shit like that again, girl," my father said, his blackening, gnarled teeth just inches from my nose. "I'll never touch you again. What I will do is tie you down and make you watch as I bend your brother over the bed. For the rest of his life, he'll question how much of a man he is, and all cuz you couldn't keep your big, fat mouth shut. Then, when I'm done with him, when he's no longer of any use to me, your sister's pretty little lips and tight, tiny twat will take his place. And you'll get to watch every time, knowing it shoulda been you. We clear?"

I knew, right then and there, that I couldn't be having a nightmare.

It wasn't because my lungs burned and teetered on the brink of explosion, and it wasn't because, any second, my windpipe would cave and I'd die. No, the truth—the reality of my situation—came because I knew, not even in the deepest corners of my own sick mind and black soul, could I come up with something so disgusting, so gut-wrenching, so evil.

That was all him.

He loosened his grip, but just a little, only enough that I could squeak out a garbled "yes" before he clenched his fingers back around my throat again, tightening them as bore heated daggers into my soul. I knew, without a doubt, he was going to kill me. And there was a brief moment, when my vision started to spot at the edges, that I actually welcomed it. No more pain. No more filth. No more evil. Just silent, endless sleep.

But then, just when I thought it might be over, he spat in my face. "Good," he growled, shoving me into the bed by my throat before releasing me. "Then tonight, you come to me. Prove you can be a good lil' girl, keep your daddy happy. Now you make yourself look real purdy for me and come knock on the next door over. One eighteen."

As I gasped and fought to fill my lungs with air, he turned to leave. I reached for him, a silent plea for him to tell me where Cole and Mya were. But the door closed behind him instead, sealing my fate, requiring me to trust that if I followed his command, my sister and brother would be okay. Untouched. Safe.

I'd like to say that I cried that night. Or that I begged

God for mercy and forgiveness. That I'd had some profound revelation, or that someone had come to save us . . . but all of that would be a bold-faced lie.

Right then and there, I'd made up my mind. I would do what needed to be done. No point in crying over it, feeling it, thinking about it. And asking for help from anyone—divine or human—wouldn't do me a damn bit of good.

No one could hear me.

No one could save me.

Not anymore.

Chapter Nineteen
The Present

San Francisco hadn't really been anything like I'd imagined it. Maybe I expected it to be more like Los Angeles. Or maybe more like further up north on the west coast. Whatever I'd expected, this wasn't it.

Or maybe, just maybe, the problem was me.

Whatever had dug its talons into my heart back in L.A. was now squeezing the ever-loving life out of me. Nothing— not the Golden Gate Bridge, the trolleys, the ocean—elicited emotion. I literally just coasted through the day, dropping Mya off at school, going to my crappy barista job, getting off, picking her up and grabbing dinner before heading back to our extended stay hotel. I didn't laugh. I didn't cry.

I just existed.

Mya's behavior lately didn't help, either. She'd started doing things completely out of character—yelling at me, throwing things, walking away from me in public places. She didn't even tell me good-bye in the mornings anymore.

I think, mostly, she was angry with me, angry that we'd left Cole, that we couldn't go back, and now it was just me and her in a crappy hotel room, literally doing nothing with our day-to-day lives.

I couldn't risk it.

I didn't have Cole's protection anymore. If our father found us . . .

But even if that weren't an issue, even if I could somehow keep us both safe while out and about, and somehow keep our location a secret from everyone, I just didn't have it in me anymore.

Case in point: the asshole tapping his fingers on the counter as I tried for the third time to get his drink right. Any second now and he might end up falling over dead from a damned heart attack.

"I'm really sorry, sir," I said, not really sorry, but also not fond of the idea of having to call in the paramedics if he started convulsing on the floor. "I promise, it'll be done in just a second."

When I finally got it right (soy instead of milk, extra caramel, no whipped cream) and set his drink up on the counter, he snatched it up with an angry sneer. "About damn time," he growled before turning on his heel and storming out the door.

I released a long, heavy sigh when the doorbell finally jingled, signaling his exit. "Miranda, my shift is up," I yelled to the back while sliding my apron over my head. "I'll see you tomorrow."

I'd' almost made it out the door when Miranda piped up from behind me. "Willow . . . Willow! Wait! Ben called in. I need you to stay."

I groaned and then clamped my eyes shut, forced myself to inhale a slow, deep breath before turning around to face my boss. I couldn't afford to lose this job. "Miranda, you know I can't," I said, brow creased in what I hoped to the gods looked apologetic. "I don't have a sitter."

Miranda pulled her coral colored lips into a heavy scowl then released a deep, heavy sigh. "I know. I know," she said. "But could you at least stay long enough for me to get someone else in. It'd be a huge help."

I glanced at my watch, staring at it for a beat while a war waged on inside my head. I did have a bit of time, and we could use the extra cash since I'd left whatever Cole had made in L.A. with him. But I didn't want to end up stuck in traffic and risk being late, either. More than that, I simply didn't feel like staying. I just wanted to go home, climb under my covers, gorge myself on chocolate, and watch The Walking Dead after Mya fell asleep.

In the end, our need for cash won out. "I can stay for ten," I said, slipping my apron back on. "After that, I have to go."

***

An extra ten minutes at work had turned into twenty. I'd bolted out the door like the coffee shop had gone up in flames, peeled out of the parking lot, only to find myself sitting at what felt like the twentieth red light in a row.

My fingers drummed over the steering wheel in rapid succession as I glanced down at the clock on the dash again. I had five more minutes to make it to Mya's school; no way in hell that was going to happen if I kept hitting every damn red light along the way.

As soon as the light turned green, I took off down the street. Just a little further . . . a few more blocks. Aaaaand another red light.

"Fuck!" I slammed the heel of my hand into the steering wheel and then, after a few more choice words, I dug in my purse for my cell phone so I could call the school and let them know I'd be late.

I might have been stubborn as hell, but even I knew when to admit to defeat.

A perky voice answered on the second ring. "Sherman Elementary."

"Yes, um, hi. This is Willow Lansing. I'm supposed to pick up Mya Lansing, and I'm running a little late."

Silence filled my ear for a moment. "I—I'm sorry, Ms. Lansing, but we had an early release day. All the children went home over an hour ago."

If I hadn't been stopped at a light, I probably would have crashed into someone. Because it took that much effort just to breathe, just to hold onto my phone, the proverbial life-line to my baby sister. "Wh—What do you mean? How did—how did she leave? Where did she go?"

"I—I'm very sorry, miss, I don't know."

I pulled the phone away from my ear, glared daggers at it as if I could somehow send my venom through the phone as I screamed at the top of my lungs. "How could you just let a little girl walk out of the school and not know where she went? I swear to gods, you better hope I find her or you're going to have a lawsuit on your hands bigger than the state of freaking Texas!"

Pissed, scared, and running on sheer adrenaline, I threw my phone into the seat next to me and peeled away from the light the second it turned green. I didn't give a fuck if a cop pulled up right behind me. They could high-speed chase me all the way to the school, for all I cared.

If Mya was gone, I'd need all the help I could get.

Chapter Twenty
The Past

"Go on, princess," dad said, smacking my ass, making me jump. He hadn't been that happy in years. "You get the first look-see at our new place."

Foot still resting on the first black stair, I stared up at the cream white exterior of the motorhome and tried to decide why it even mattered anymore. Or why he even acted like he cared.

Three years. Three long years of drifting from one town to the next, holing up in hotels when we could afford them and camping out in the woods when we couldn't. Why this? Why now?

As I finally hoisted myself inside, I decided it didn't matter. This would be just like the rest of my life. The inside of this camper would be no different from the inside of the hotels or the camping tents. It would become a tomb. A place where I would sacrifice myself, each and every night, for the sake of my siblings. A place where my soul—or what little was left of it—would die just a little more until, eventually, his disease devoured me completely.

I knew it would happen. I'd known the night I'd gone to him in his room, stripped myself down and willingly fell to his feet. It'd been a hefty price—my soul for Cole and Mya's—but it was one I'd paid willingly. And maybe that was somehow better than him stealing it. At least my willingness gave me power, a little sliver of control, something to hold onto so I didn't drown.

I would need that little something, that tiny part of myself that still existed somewhere deep inside. I'd hidden it far away from him, away from the world, and even from myself. I didn't know when or how, but it would be the one thing that saved us all. Because if there's one thing I knew, it was that my penance in no way guaranteed Mya and Cole's safety. Not for good. Not forever. And I sure as hell wouldn't stand idly by when he finally decided I wasn't enough anymore.

"I'll teach you to drive it," he said, coming up behind me as I opened up the cupboards above the sink. "We can go see all kinds of places in this. The Grand Canyon. The ocean. Wherever."

I turned to face him and leaned against the counter. "What's with the bonding crap all of a sudden?" I asked, sweeping my narrowed gaze over him, fully aware that I'd stepped out of line. "It's not like you're up for the father of the year award."

I noticed the tick in his jaw a hair of a second before the right side of my face started burning with pain. A year or two ago, my hand probably would have went straight to my cheek to rub the place where he'd just punched me, but I wouldn't give him the satisfaction. Not that day. Not on the anniversary of my mother's death, of the night he stolen everything from me.

"Goin' get smart now, ain't we?" he spat, stepping toe-to-

toe with me, looming over me, trying to force me to cower in his shadow.

I steeled my jaw and lifted my chin. "I want to know what your angle is. What do you even care what I think? What Cole or Mya thinks? You've never cared before. Why now?"

Before I could even blink, his hands were tangled in the hair at the nape of my neck. He yanked my head at an angle as he dragged me through the cabin. "Why you ungrateful little . . . " He shoved me onto the bed in the back, sending me face first onto the mattress.

I flopped onto my back and scooted myself back across the unmade bed, trying to put some distance between me and his wrath.

The corner of his mouth lifted in a maniacal grin. "Cole! Mya! Get on in here," he yelled, holding my gaze as he undid his belt, sliding it from the loops. "You gone and did it now, girl," he muttered.

I watched in horror when Cole and then Mya stepped up into the trailer just as he dropped his jeans to the ground. Gods, he wouldn't. He couldn't. Not here. Not now. Not in front of them. "Daddy, please," I begged, tears filling my eyes for the first time in years. "Don't do this."

"Do what, princess?" He climbed onto the bed, closing the distance between us. "Show your sister and brother what a whore you are? How much you love to please your daddy? What they're going to do when I get damn sick and tired of your smart little mouth?"

My eyes flitted back and forth between my father's approaching form and Cole and Mya, standing in the doorway, watching with wide-eyed horror. I couldn't breathe past the fear choking the life out of me, the humiliation that consumed me. Couldn't hear past the sobs and sniffles filling the small space. Couldn't see anything other than my target, the wrinkly but erect appendage just below my foot. If I could just . . .

"Get off!" Cole's shrill scream scraped against my ear drums. "Get off of her!"

My gaze shot to Cole, who was standing just at the edge of the bed. It took all but a second to register what had happened, why my father had stopped his advance. Why he hovered over me with an open mouth and wide, fear-filled eyes.

"Cole . . . " I soothed, soft and low, careful not to move too quickly, afraid that the gun pressed to my father's temple would go off if I did. "Please, honey. Put it down."

"No, Willow. I—I can't." Cole shook his head and the gun moved slightly, singeing my chest with another pang of panic. "I won't let him do this anymore. I saw him, what he did. To you. To momma. He's not going to hurt anyone anymore."

"Cole, if you do this, if you pull that trigger, you're no better than he is," I said, slowly sliding myself out from underneath my father, closer to my brother. "You're better than that. You're better than him."

"But he hurt you. He hurt momma," Cole said, turning

his tear-filled eyes on me. "He'll just hurt someone else. What if he hurts me? Or Mya? He will, you know? He just said he would."

"No, bubba, he won't." I said, finally close enough to slowly reach for my brother's shaky hands. "I'll make sure he doesn't." Certain that even breathing would break the spell, I held the air in my lungs and carefully wrapped my fingers over the barrel. "I promise. I'll keep you safe. I'll keep Mya safe. Just let go, please."

A sob escaped Cole's throat as he finally released the gun, leaving the weight of it in my hands. The cold metal felt soothing against my sweaty palms, grounded me, gave me confidence as I scooted the rest of the way off the bed and then rose to stand at the foot of it.

"Good girl," my father said, his blanched face relaxing just a little. "Now, go on, give me that damn thing 'fore someone gets hurt."

I swallowed, hard, and then bit at my lower lip, weighing my options.

If this piece of shit died, no one would miss him. I could carry the weight of his death on my shoulders. Hell, I might even hold my head high knowing that the man who'd taken so much from me—from everyone—had finally gotten what he deserved. But then Mya tugged at my pant leg, reminding me that I wasn't alone, that this wasn't just about me. Never had been.

And that meant I had to do the right thing.

"No, I'm not going to do that, Amos," I said, intentionally

refusing to call him my father. "What I *am* going to do is drive this rig out of here with Cole and Mya. And you're not coming with us."

His laugh grated down my spine like a million tiny needles. "You can't drive this thing, girl. What are you thinkin'? And how 'bout money? School? You gonna take care of those two leeches all on yer lil' lonesome?"

I grit my teeth, forced myself to breath deep through my nose, fought the urge to argue with the devil. "That's for me to worry about," I clipped, spreading my stance, rolling my shoulders back to prepare for the worst.

"Oh, and what're ya' gonna do if I refuse to go?" he asked, narrowing his eyes at me, at the gun pointed straight at his head.

I tilted my head to the side and smiled with so much saccharine sweetness, it made my own stomach hurt. "I'll shoot you in the dick," I said, redirecting my aim. I let it sink in for a moment, waited until his throat bobbed with a heavy swallow. Then, and only then did I let the grin slide off my lips.

"You wouldn't," he whispered, tiny beads of sweat coating his bushy brow.

"Oh, but I would. Now get up." I waved the gun in the direction of the door. "Get your pants and get the hell out of here."

His eyelid twitched as he watched me for a moment, probably analyzing me, sizing me up, trying to decide if I'd really pull the trigger. In the end, he must have decided I just might.

"You'll pay for this," he seethed as he slid off the bed, grabbed his pants, and then made his way to the door. "You just wait, girl. You'll pay. That little sister of yours, she'll make a nice little replacement for you. And when I get a hold of her, you'll never find her again."

My finger itched, begged me to squeeze. I fought against it by keeping Mya's red curls and Cole's heaving shoulders in my view. They needed me, and that was all that mattered. The only thing that ever had. And now I could keep them safe. I *would* keep them safe.

No matter what it took.

No matter what I had to give up along the way.

I would keep my promise.

Chapter Twenty-One
The Present

I brought my car to a screeching halt outside the school. Not even bothering to kill the engine, I flung the driver's side door open, took off in a sprint up to the front doors, grabbed the metal handle and yanked . . . but the door didn't budge.

I tried all the other doors, but each and every damn one of them was locked.

"Hey!" I screamed, using the heel of my hand to pound on the glass. "Is anyone in there? Please! Please! Someone open the door!"

I don't know how long I kept banging. I have no idea how long I screamed at the top of my lungs. But by the time I finally stopped, my throat had gone hoarse. Not that I really even noticed.

The only thing I really noticed was the way it felt like I'd fallen into some sort of dream state, like none of this could be real. Because it couldn't be. There was no way that Mya had gone missing.

There just wasn't.

Yet, there I stood, the fog crowding around me, suffocating me—or maybe that had just been my imagination. It certainly didn't feel like it. No, it felt like something very real had slunk down my throat and into my chest, had somehow grasped a hold of my lungs and was now trying to pull them up and out of my windpipe, along with my heart and stomach.

Somehow, I managed to find my way back to the car, had driven down every single street in a five mile radius, hoping that maybe she'd simply walked to one of the nearby shops to wait for me. When that turned up nothing, I parked the car, started walking inside of the stores that I thought might appeal to her most. Still nothing.

With each passing second, I knew my chances of finding her were slimming. And by the time the setting sun started to cast its orange glow over the bay, I knew . . . I would never see her again.

I could call Cole, ask him to drive up there and come help me find her, tell him how epically I'd fucked things up . . . but even if he drove straight to San Francisco, it'd be too late by the time he arrived.

No, the reality was, we'd never find her, not now, not hours after she'd disappeared. Our father had won. He'd kept his promise.

And I'd failed to keep mine.

Cole would never forgive me.

I'd never forgive myself.

The End

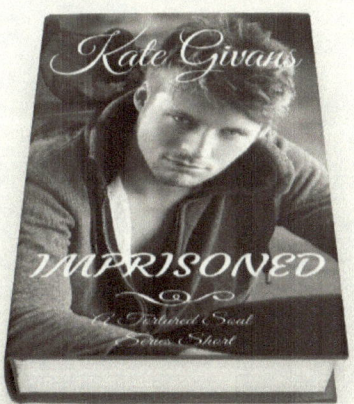

Acknowledgements

I swear, this gets harder each time . . . but it also gets a little easier because there is always that amazing group of people that stand behind you, no matter how rough the waters get. For me, those people are my amazing beta readers, Heidi and Kylie. I couldn't do this without you ladies. Kimberly and Stace, you're now added to that amazing bunch! Thank you for joining my amazing circle of trusted friends. You ladies have no idea how much it means to me that you're willing to look at the roughest form of my work and still tell me you love it.

Rach, my bestie and now "official" Twisted Sister, I don't think I ever would have hit publish if it weren't for you. I'll always be grateful for those words spoken in the SeaTac airport elevator. They changed my life, as have you. Love you to the moon and back again!

To my Book Club, you ladies rock my world, each and every day! Thank you for taking a chance on an Indie author you didn't know and showing me exactly how amazing the book community can really be!

To all my blogger friends and readers, YOU make the world go 'round. Without you, my stories are nothing more than my own crazy on a page. Thanks for making me feel welcome in such an amazing world.

To my children and my husband, James: I know I hide away, sometimes in a full house in my writing spot and you all probably wonder if I even know you're there when I'm lost in my own head, speaking for my characters. I do. And I love you so much for being so wonderfully supportive and understanding as I pursue a dream I never thought would be real. Thank you for encouraging me, for putting up with me, and for loving this crazy person you call wife an mom.

Miranda, my Jellybean, I miss you! And you are so much stronger than you know. I think you're finally seeing it, so please don't forget!

Liz, you're going to get through this. And I love you.

Morgan, you have got to be one of the strongest women I have ever met. It's no wonder my brother fell for you! I know you miss him terribly. I'd give anything to make it hurt just a little less.

Bella-Bean, you are perfect and amazing and remind me SO much of your daddy!

And to the dreamers, the wanderers, the lost and broken - you are not alone.

www.ingramcontent.com/pod-product-compliance
Lightning Source LLC
Chambersburg PA
CBHW030542130626
46552CB00006B/2379